Over the Rooftops of Time

Jewish
Stories
Essays
Poems

Myra Sklarew

STATE UNIVERSITY OF NEW YORK PRESS

Cover art by Lithuanian artist Aleksandra Jacovskaite.

Published by
STATE UNIVERSITY OF NEW YORK PRESS
Albany

© 2003 State University of New York

For information, address
State University of New York Press
90 State Street, Suite 700, Albany, NY 12207

Production and book design, Laurie Searl
Marketing, Fran Keneston

Library of Congress Cataloging-in-Publication Data

Sklarew, Myra.
    Over the rooftops of time: Jewish stories, essays, poems/by Myra
    Sklarew.
       p. cm.—(SUNY series in modern Jewish literature and culture)
    Includes index.
    ISBN 0-7914-5575-0 (acid-free paper)—ISBN 0-7914-5576-9
    (pbk: acid-free paper)
    1. Judaism—Literary collections. 2. Jews—Literary collections.
3. Judaism. 4. Jews. I. Title. II. Series.

PS3569.K57 O94 2002
818'.5409—dc21
                                                          2002017731

10   9   8   7   6   5   4   3   2   1

Over the

Rooftops of Time

SUNY series in

MODERN JEWISH LITERATURE AND CULTURE

Sarah Blacher Cohen, editor

this book is dedicated with love

to a trio of precious granddaughters

Rachel, Allison, Danielle

Contents

Acknowledgments

Grateful acknowledgment is made to the publications in which these stories, essays, and poems originally appeared:

American University: "Crossing into the New Millennium"; *Azul Editions*: "Then," "Crossing Over," "Ode to the Czar's Assassin," "The Messiah Reconsidered," "On Muranowka Street"; *B'nai B'rith International Jewish Monthly*: "The Landscape of Dislocation," "Learning the Language," "Who Has Not Dreamed of Flying?" "Morocco: Gauze Curtains, Round Tombs," "My Companion the Aleph-Bet," "The Roots of Resistance"; *Dryad Press*: "From the Backyard of the Diaspora," "What Hasanin M'Barak Said," "Holocaust," "Instructions for the Messiah," "What Is a Jewish Poem?"; *Rubber City, European Judaism*: "1941"; *International Herald Tribune*: "At the Heart of Transplant Surgery"; *Jewish Book Annual, Jewish Book Council*: "Yiddish Poetry"; *Keshev Publishing House*: "Night Watch"; *Lost Roads Publishers*: "In the Afterlife Which Is a Library," "The Messenger," "Getting There," "Like a Field Riddled by Ants," "Certainty"; *Nature Medicine*, 1995, Vol. 1, pp. 959–960, "Genes, Blood and Courage: A Boy Called Immortal Sword by David Nathan"; *Sifrut*: "Writing the Holocaust: *auch ohne/Sprache*"; *Three Continents Press*: "Khamsin"; *Tuftonia*: "A Journal for John Holmes"; *Washington Post Book Review*: "The Puzzle People"; *Washington Post Magazine*: "Counterpoint"; *Washington Review of the Arts*: "Interview with Joseph Brodsky," "The Howard Poets in Perspective."

"In the Afterlife Which is a Library" and "Getting There" received the PEN Syndicated Fiction Award. *From the Backyard of the Diaspora* received the DiCastagnola Award from the Poetry Society of America and the Jewish Book Council Award in Poetry. "Lithuania" received the Anna Davidson Rosenberg Award from the Judah Magnes Museum. A portion of the writings have been recorded for the Library of Congress's Archives of Poetry and Literature.

Grateful thanks to Marianna Volkov for use of her photograph of Joseph Brodsky; to Lithuanian artists Adomas Jacovskis for "Hesitating Bird," his sister Aleksandra Jacovskaite for the cover art—consummate, unique talents; to my sister Janice Eanet who has since childhood helped me to live; to my sister Betsy Buxer who has always led the way, and for her work in arranging the final manuscript and helping to release material that did not belong; to B.S., friend of forty-eight years. I thank Carla Shatz and Lief Finkel for permission to quote from their writings, both inspiring explorers on the frontiers of neuroscience; Aharon Megged for permission to quote from his moving writings; Charles Fenyvesi for encouraging the writing of essays that appeared in the B'nai B'rith International Jewish Monthly, and for giving me twenty-seven minutes to decide, in 1980, to go to Morocco; my daughter Deborah who was about to be married for telling me to do it, and to the editors of the publications listed here who took a risk on a writer who is still learning her way. I thank Sarah Blacher Cohen, inspiring, talented mentor and joyful apprehender of life who erases obstacles before they have a chance to fully surface. Special love to Eric and Renee, Deborah and Mark.

Preface

It is said that the Jewish homeland is alive in time. That each of us is poured like the contents of a vessel from Sinai to here. That even those not yet born will bear the inscription of Sinai. Whether the subject in these essays is language or memory, the intent is to provide a trace of that homeland. S. Y. Agnon tells the fable of a goat whose milk is so sweet it is a balm to the bones of an old man. But the goat keeps disappearing. The son sets out to follow the goat to discover where she goes. Eventually they come to a cave and when they emerge the son asks where this place is that is full of the choicest fruit and a "fountain of living waters." "The land of Israel," he is told, "close by Safed." The story ends sadly; the easy way to the Land of Israel is closed off. "The mouth of the cave has been hidden from the eye." Spiritual loss and exile are the order of the day.

These essays tell of the remaining Jewish communities of Morocco; the Lithuanian Holocaust; a search for the birthplace of a grandfather; a woman's struggle to embrace Judaism; resistance in the French town of Le Chambon; exile of the body in illness and the potential for healing through gene therapy and stem cell research. Like Isaac Singer's portrayal of his most ordinary men and women in their vanished shtetl worlds dreaming their extraordinary dreams, it is hoped that these remnants will permit us to imagine the larger fabric of which they are made. Perhaps our narrator, like Isaac Singer's Yasha the magician of Lublin, can also achieve flight. Perhaps she can gain access to the forbidden—whether it is against gravity she pits herself or against a tradition that for so long kept women on the other side of the *machitza,* the partition, tucked safely under their *sheitels,* their marriage wigs. Our flight may be like the bee's, aeronautically unsound, but doable, permitting us at long last to become full participants. To point to the words of the Torah ourselves. And perhaps this flying can be not only away from but toward. An embrace.

Perhaps the single most important issue of our new century is whether the instinctual side of humankind will be kept in check or whether it will, as we have seen so clearly in recent days, erupt with murderous force. How can individual, parental, or cultural influences enhance our ability to sublimate our aggressive drives? In these works, this question is the reigning principle. As I believe it to be the main tenet of Judaism and the central Talmudic principle—a set of doctrines, flexible in nature, to govern our behavior. Writings sufficiently cognizant of human nature to remain valid and of use for the duration of time. Writings which contain the legal codes, *halakhah,* and superb illustrations, *aggadah,* story that is, according to Bialik, "the crucible of the *halakhah.*"

I want to offer amnesty for those readers averse to science, but with a warning. The changes in science and medicine affect each of us. Drug resistance and the search for effective alternatives to the known antibiotics; the burgeoning cases of HIV infection—in Zimbabwe today one in three persons is infected; the difficult ethical issues posed by our increasing knowledge of the role of genetics in treating illnesses and in aiding reproduction; the use of viruses as vectors in treating disease; the enormous strides made in the neurosciences; and the advent of transplantation are subjects worthy of our attention and thought.

On a more personal note, childhood illness and the threat of rheumatic heart disease as a consequence of untreated strep infections—there was no viable treatment at the time—kept me away from school and isolated for long periods. The combination of reading through my parents' library, wandering about in the woods near our home, and spending time in my biochemist father's laboratory, created in me an attentiveness to the natural world and to the world of science. The discovery of penicillin had a direct impact on my life, ending the years of isolation. Back then I took to growing bread mold on the windowsills of our house, urging the gray-green products of my experimentation upon my younger sister who, despite my ministrations, managed to survive!

Though I have kept the various areas of my life separated, it makes no sense to maintain artificial partitions any longer. Just as the years of specialization and development in individual areas of science, once the barriers were removed, have resulted in biochemists, geneticists, molecular biologists, physicists, bio-engineers working together to solve many of the medical/biological questions of our day, so does it seem sensible in an individual life to permit art and science to cohabit. In the arts we learn about process, about the underlying feeling state, about symbolic thought. Creative process may be applied to all areas of study and knowledge. A single image or a momentary suspension of time may be the key that unlocks a lifetime of questioning. Noble laureate Gerald Edelman, during an airport delay, sketched out an entire theory of memory formation based on a lifetime of work in immunology. Just as the artist gives credence to a recurring image, or a language phrase, or a line of music, so for the filmmaker, as Ingmar Bergman once described it, a year-long recurring image of four women in a room whose walls were red, became the basis for his masterwork, *Cries and Whispers*. Artists and scientists can privilege attentiveness to images or ideas transposed from one field to another, for example, investigating the display of the unconscious in dreaming. A wonderful illustration of this is chemist F. A. Kekule's struggle to discover the structure of benzene. Prior to his discovery, molecular structures were conceived as linear. He dreamed of forms turning like serpents until one "seized its own tail" and he suddenly visualized the benzene ring, a hexagonal structure.

For years I have kept the elements of my life apart, as one holds apart two walls. It has been written that when two walls collapse, as they are falling they form a bridge. May this collection be such a bridge. Science, poetry, religion, and language, companions, our earth, the ancient and the immediate, the known and what is unknowable—all talking at once in these pages. And may those who overhear this conversation feel themselves to be included.

Learning the Language

THE LANDSCAPE OF DISLOCATION

*T*here are no troops marching along our borders. I do not hear the sounds of German or Russian or Czech, of French, Italian, or Polish. Only the inexact rendering of the language into which I was born: English. The language my mother, the daughter of immigrants, so cherished. She would be dismayed to learn how uncommunicative it has become, how abstract and full of jargon.

So unlike the flavor of the language of the old Greek woman whose house I once lived in. Yiayia peering down at me from an upper-story window of a century-old Boston house as I carried my infant son about. Yiayia, saying in Greek with her index finger curled in front of her face: *Ta pouli, Mira, ta pouli,* referring to his tiny penis as a little bird, her finger mocking, her voice sharp, the face wicked, teasing—a village face. *Ta pouli,* her fingers fly the little bird away. Yiayia had raised eight children in a Greek mountain village while her husband, roaming America to make his fortune, didn't, and hadn't the courage or money to return to Greece. Finally, the eldest son left Greece and came to find his father, to bring his old parents together again.

Yiayia liked to tell how she stayed at home with the roosters while her husband in America played around with the

3

chickens. Sometimes she would squat by the kitchen table to show us how she had given birth to each child, grunting and smiling to reassure us, then shaking her head at the memory she had stirred inside herself. Though neither she nor her husband Pappou could read, they knew history and remembered with great precision all they had lived through, from the Turkish occupation to their own civil war in which brother fought against brother and children walked past dead and familiar bodies on the way to school.

Yiayia and Pappou relished their reconciliation. In an attic apartment at the top of the house, they resided like aging royalty, cheating each other at cards and generally interfering in the lives of their children. The eldest son and his wife took care of them as was the absolute custom, and the old woman cooked in her daughter-in-law's kitchen, spoiling the children and contradicting all the rules the younger woman set while the eldest son worked his long hours in a restaurant downtown. They always waited up for him to come home, all of them. Waited to have their strong Turkish coffee—one of the few Turkish influences they acceded to—at one in the morning. Afterward, Yiayia would turn the little cups over in order to read our fortunes in the thick grounds which hardened on the inside curve of the cup. For her unmarried son Dimitri she saw a comely *yunaika,* a woman; for her married son *lepta,* money; for her daughter-in-law, who had already produced four children, she saw *paidia,* more children. Her predictions seldom varied. We would tease her about this but she would just grin her toothless grin and shake her head as though to point out our foolishness for questioning an old woman's ability.

I remember a day when I went up the back stairs and, looking through the glass transom, was stunned to see the two men, Dimitri and Michael, with their arms raised up over their heads, their faces contorted in rage, and Toula—Michael's wife—the recipient of such passion. Were they about to strike her? Each other? Suddenly they caught sight of me at their door. The arms drew down magically, the faces smiled, the heads bowed. I heard through the door their courtly invitation to join them. "We were just having a little discussion," they told me. Later, only later, was I allowed to share in their political discussions, later when I was part of the family, trusted. Thinking of this now, I am reminded of the sign Dino Skenderis put up in his grocery store during the military regime in Greece: No Talking about Politics.

Why do I think of this Greek family when I stare at the empty wall in front of me where I have dragged my desk? And why do I keep my desk in an empty corner rather than look out each day onto old trees and suburban yards, automobiles readied in the driveways, split-rail fences, sturdy houses, construction, a good road full of traffic day and night, the small whir as comforting and familiar as the air conditioners that hum all summer.

Why am I so struck by the words of T. Carmi, the Israeli poet who was born in America: "There were poets who took refuge in childhood memories, writing from behind closed shutters in Tel Aviv or Jerusalem, just as the early painters in the bare Judean or Galilee hills continued to inhabit an imaginary cloud-filled Ecole de Paris." Do I somehow not trust this landscape I have been born into? Is this the reverse of Carmi's poets, who could not tolerate in their arts geographical dislocation? As David Shimoni writes in his poem: "A blossoming winter contrived to entice me/ but I dreamed of the deserts of snow."

And if I were taken from my familiar landscape, which I do not look out on, would I suffer a secondary dislocation? Would I only then long for it, paint it into my poems in its absence?

To go back, why do I romanticize my adopted Greek family, learn their language and customs, learn how to cook their food, incorporate their folklore as though it were my own: "The good pappou resides above, the bad pappou below," the old man tells the children, belt in hand, when they are obstreperous. They plead with him not to release the evil pappou from the cellar. He winks at me, other things on his mind. "My passion," he tells me, "is as rotten as that artichoke spoiling on the table." "More *pouli*," the old woman clucks, shooting him a look. I think to myself how his impotence is transferred directly into his power over this herd of children, which he daily pulls and cajoles into line. Children with that unadulterated energy partial to the offspring of immigrants. Children willful and determined to do better than their parents. Determined to become Americans. And to be educated. Above all.

And why do I suddenly think of the town where I lived during my adolescence, whose adults had been born in Italy and Poland and Czechoslovakia? The children were my schoolmates. I did not know then that it was an unusual town. I did not think about the music I shared with these boys and girls, the Czech folk songs, the Italian love songs and arias we sang on the bus every Friday night on the way back from basketball games, our school's only sport. It did not seem unusual to play in a dance band with these same friends for the local Polish and Czech dance halls so that the adults could come together to dance their national dances. I thought somehow that this was just a typical town.

It is difficult to integrate the two lives, the suburban with one with strong ties to a European base, a "foreign" family speaking another language, living by certain abiding forms. I am reminded of the friend who struggles to make room in his life for a woman he loves and her children, when the need for space—physical as well as emotional—is all-consuming. I wonder what has become of the various forms by which we once gave each other room.

I remember a story my mother told me a long time ago. When her uncle came to this country from Lithuania, after a long and painful separation, he was able to bring his family here, one by one. When the final member of the family arrived—his youngest daughter, by this time a young woman—not a single word was exchanged. She knelt down and the father placed his hands over her head and blessed her. Such was their greeting.

I think of Bialik the poet and the cold dark mornings when his *matmid*—talmudic student—arose and went to his dark corner to pray and pore over Talmud and Torah, the appropriate prayer on his tongue, the ritual guiding him in his behavior toward his God and toward those with whom he shared his life. Though his small room might become crowded, one soul did not intrude upon the other. There was room for all.

A number of years back—I don't remember just how many anymore—I met the son of a Yiddish poet whose work I had read. The poet was Halpern Leivick—that visionary figure who stood at the center of modern Yiddish poetry. He was born in Ihumen, a small town in Byelorussia, and had been driven into exile in Siberia for activity in the socialist Bund. He arrived in the United States in 1913. It seemed nearly incomprehensible to me that he could have a living son and that son could live here, barely a mile away. Though we did not meet often, I felt a great warmth toward that son Daniel and his wife and relished seeing them. Two occasions stand out. The first was an afternoon spent around the Leivick's dining room table with Cynthia Ozick; we were translating a poem by Daniel's father, a lullaby. We each tried to write a version of the poem and then put together our various attempts, combining the most successful phrases and lines. I remember a lengthy discussion about how to translate a certain Yiddish word, which meant plaything or toy, into English. We finally settled on the word *thimble*.

It was a sweet afternoon. A room with four adults sitting together, laboring over a shared task, moving the father's lullaby across the barrier of language, moving it toward us word by word.

Later, when my own mother was dying, we came across a letter her father had written to her mother when she had gone to visit relatives in a distant city. It was written in Yiddish. I took the letter to Daniel, and he and his wife helped to decipher it. It was an unusual letter; my grandfather spoke to his wife with great affection and respect, with a kind of formal dignity that surprised me. Somehow it did not match the picture I had carried around inside for so many years of the hard-working, gruff man who had fathered eight children, five surviving daughters, two sons. The protective, religious, early-exhausted man, my grandfather whose name I bear, had died before I was born. What remains in my mind now is the picture I have of that afternoon when Daniel and Ida sat together explaining gently the words of his letter, which I carefully wrote down so that I would not forget one thing when I told my mother who waited at home for this last bit of news of her father and mother.

What has this to do with the suburbs? Is it possible to live in a place, not a mile from someone without discovering when that person dies? Not until midwinter did I learn that in the fall Daniel had died suddenly one morning. I found out only by accident, talking by telephone long distance to someone about another matter entirely. It is possible to live side by side with one another and rarely meet. It is possible not to share the most significant events of each other's lives. I am as much to blame as anyone.

Sometimes, when I feel particularly disquieted by this life, I imagine that I am walking in the old city in Jerusalem. I know for certain at those moments that I am no longer in the suburbs. Perhaps the real suburb is only a name for a state of mind that represents a removal from the central district or village, a dislocation from what is human, a removal from the heart. We hold on, barely: centripetal force keeps us here.

From the Backyard of the Diaspora

So I say
that we are enclosed here
by more than history
or barbed wire or chimneys

but by these small yards
by the absence of mountains
by our own immobility
which straps us
to the distance
that moves to the west
and away from us.

You send blessings
from Jerusalem.

They are old
and arrive at night
like the stirring
of birds in a dream.
Within the moist cave
of my body
I call back.

In the exile of this landscape
there are no Babylonians,
no Assyrians,
only this split-rail fence
over which the dogwood leans
in spring
as though it were
about to speak.

LEARNING THE LANGUAGE

*F*or many years I have tried to learn Hebrew. I have studied conversational Hebrew (*Habet Ushma*), Hebrew for travelers, total immersion Hebrew, Hebrew for schoolchildren, Hebrew for beginners, Hebrew for beginning adults, painless Hebrew, painful Hebrew, prayer Hebrew, Hebrew in the marketplace, Hebrew and the holidays, Hebrew for Israelis.

In addition, I have often needed to clarify some point or other in the Bible, but my knowledge of the Bible was insufficient. I could never find exactly what I was looking for with any haste. I was put in touch with a fellow, an Israeli, who was principal of a religious school. Noach, I would say, quick tell me, what does Job say to his friends when they come to advise him? He would answer immediately. He knew the Bible by heart. One day I said, Noach, I need a teacher. I want to learn Hebrew. Let me think about it, he said. Call me tomorrow. I waited the long day and called the next. I have just the person for you, Noach told me. Good, I say. Who is it? My wife, he replied.

My teacher's name was Bracha—blessing. She would be my guide, my Virgil in the ascent from the darkness of ignorance to the celestial heights of the Hebrew root to which I would attach prefixes and suffixes. I would embellish the language of my people. Soon there would be sentences, entire paragraphs and, who knows, maybe someday beautiful poems, *piyutim* fit for the synagogue.

The grandmothers and great-grandmothers who had flown above us during my son's bar mitzvah would be pleased that I had finally learned the language. In the afterlife they would already be making room on the shelves of the great library for the poetry I would translate, the books of Genesis and Exodus, the poetry of Ibn Gabirol, and Yehuda Halevi and Shmuel HaNagid, the commentaries of the rabbis.

It was my plan to begin my study of Hebrew by reading the poetry of contemporary Israelis, some of whom I had met and corresponded with. I could not forget the first time I heard Hebrew spoken not for purposes of prayer in the synagogue but in the recitation of modern poetry by the Israeli writer Yehuda Amichai. At first I thought he must be praying, but then I realized he was reciting a poem and that it contained words that belonged to contemporary life, words like *automobile, bomb, God* with a small *g*.

I said to my teacher, Now I will read the poetry of my Israeli friend in his language. Now, I said. This day. Sure, she said. Okay, she said. But first we will begin with Abraham and Sarah and Isaac.

I had meant my friend Amichai, and Moshe Dor and Carmi and Kovner. She understood perfectly: Genesis. So for all of one summer I trudged along imperfectly behind Abraham as he walked hand in hand with his son Isaac toward Mount Moriah. I observed how the father did not raise his eyes from the ground. I listened as he answered the son's question, partway on the journey: "And Isaac spoke unto Abraham his father and said, My father. And he said, Here am I, my son"—just as Abraham had responded when God spoke to him. And he said, "Behold the fire and the wood, but where is the lamb for a burnt offering?" And Abraham said, "God will provide Himself the lamb for a burnt offering, my son. So they went both of them together"—words that gain increasing poignancy as the passage continues. Here we witness that most supreme test of faith, the offering up by Abraham of his most precious possession, his child, and we witness the beginning of the end of human sacrifice.

Later, the themes set forth in this biblical passage will serve poets of our own age, yet the meaning changes; the new poem based on the binding of Isaac will have to include the Holocaust, as in "Isaac," by the Israeli poet Amir Gilboa:

At dawn, the sun strolled in the forest
together with me and father
and my right hand was in his left.
Like lightning a knife flashed among the trees.
And I am so afraid of my eyes' terror
faced by blood on the leaves.
Father, father, quickly save Isaac
so that no one will be missing at the midday meal.
It is I who am being slaughtered, my son,
and already my blood is on the leaves.
And father's voice was smothered and his face was
    pale.
And I wanted to scream, writhing not to believe
and tearing open my eyes
and I woke up.
And my right hand was drained of blood.[1]

The poem has reversed the biblical account, explains the Israeli scholar Arieh Sachs. The knife flashing between the trees threatens both father and son; the blood on the leaves refers to the massacres in the forests of Eastern Europe. The poet, his family, his people are victims of something that is hardly comprehensible as a trial of faith. The language of reenactment has been bent and torn to fit the nightmare, Sachs concludes.[2]

    The next summer I said to my teacher, Bracha: I will learn to read Hebrew poetry. Yes, she said, of course you will. We will study Bialik. I thought wistfully of my friend Yehuda Amichai sitting in his rooms at Yemin Moshe looking out toward the Tower of David. I thought of Carmi and Moshe Dor and Kovner. Bialik it was, all that summer.

    It is with Chaim Nahman Bialik that Hebrew finds its modern voice and in the process rediscovers important chapters of its long history. The transition of Hebrew from its center in 1890 in Odessa to its new home in Palestine by 1920 affected the music, themes, and locales of Hebrew poetry. It is a remarkable achievement that Bialik was able to provide Hebrew poetry with a new idiom that fused together the various strata of language. Because of the absence of living speech these strata tended to remain separate. Bialik's poetry seemed to recapitulate successive stages of Jewish history.

My teacher Bracha and I waited inside the pages of his poetry for the Talmud student to arrive. He did not disappoint us, but came to the Yeshiva to study, came while it was still dark, sitting in the lonely room before the world ever arose.

His long poem "HaMatmid," translated by Maurice Samuel, begins this way:

> There are abandoned corners of our exile.
> Remote forgotten cities of Dispersion,
> Where still in secret burns our ancient light,
> Where God has saved a remnant from disaster . . .
> And when thou goest forth alone, at nightfall
> Wandering in one of these, the sacred cities,
> When heaven above is quick with breaking stars
> And earth beneath with whispering spirit-winds,
> Thine ear will catch the murmur of a voice,
> And a human form . . .
> A shadow trembling, swaying back and forth
> A voice that lifts and falls and comes toward thee
> upon the waves of silence,
> Mark well the swaying shadow and the voice.
> It is a Matmid in his prison-house,
> A prisoner, self-guarded, self-condemned,
> Self-sacrificed to study of the Law . . .[3]

Bracha and I did not finish our reading of the poem that summer just as Bialik did not resolve the conflict of that poem—the exalted vision of the devoted student—or answer the terrible question: To what end is this mighty sacrifice?

One of my favorite poems by Bialik is about a violin to whom the poet tells all the secrets of his heart but the poet dies—his life stops in the middle before he has had a chance to sing the rest of the song of his life, and, therefore, one string of the violin remains mute and waiting for him though he doesn't come. This is how I translated it, with Bracha's help: "There was a man and see he isn't anymore and the song of his life stopped in the middle; another *shir mizmor* he had and behold, lost is the *mizmor,* forever lost."

Finally, the next summer I said emphatically: Bracha, this summer I want to study Hebrew poetry—Amichai, Carmi, Dor, Shlonsky, Uri Zvi Greenberg. Yes, she said at last. Yes, patiently. Choose a book by Amichai. Let us have a look.

Now, I thought, when I reconstructed the pattern of these Hebrew lessons, just what is Hebrew poetry? A poetic literature written in a language spanning the centuries from King Solomon to Kovner, a language basically little different now from what it was in the time of Solomon. A miraculous living language. None other has survived in this way.

To understand Hebrew poetry, we might begin with Biblical poetry, going to medieval *piyutim*, to Yiddish poetry, to contemporary Israeli poetry, but the movement, the development was not linear. Rather, it traveled geographically as well as through time, stilled at its center in Palestine for a time, then developing and altering itself in Spain, Turkey, Italy, Africa, Greece.

Aharon Megged, the Israeli novelist, has summed it up this way:

> The revival of the Hebrew language is not like Lazarus arising miraculously from the dead. It is more like Sleeping Beauty awakened by the Prince. She was not dead, she had only been dormant for a long time; and she was not rotten bones but a real beauty. Now when you betroth her and bring her into your house, your problem is how to make this noble, aristocratic princess, adorned with jewels and clad in purple, do all the domestic work, soil her hands, break her back cooking, washing and tending the garden in the backyard. Contrary to Eliza Doolittle of Pygmalion, she is quite all right in fancy parties but she misbehaves in the marketplace.[4]

The marketplace, according to T. Carmi, was Palestine. There, he tells us, Hebrew poetry faced one of its harshest trials: the need to adjust to a new geography, to a Mediterranean texture of light and seasons and sounds. That this landscape was also familiar, that these hills and rivers had been sung before by poets who had inhabited them in real life or in the life of the imagination, was both an advantage and an impediment. The literary memory had to make way for fresh, immediate vision.

Aharon Megged said:

> I remember myself as a school boy, sitting in the classroom in the small village where I grew up, reading Chapter 37 in

Genesis, all about Joseph and his brethren. While reading how Joseph being 17 years old was feeding his father's flock together with the sons of Bilha and Zilpa and wearing a striped coat, I looked through the window and saw the Arab shepherd boys, also feeding their flock and wearing striped gowns. It all merged into one haze, and I could not tell what was real and what was narrative. Look at the book, the teacher rebuked me. But which was the book?[5]

Abraham Shlonsky wrote: "My land is wrapped in light as in a prayer shawl. The houses stand forth like phylacteries. Here the lovely city says the morning prayer to its Creator. And among the creators is your son Abraham, a road-building bard in Israel."

I no longer remember where I first encountered the words by Abba Kovner, the Israeli poet who, as head of the United Partisan Organization in Vilna, Lithuania, after the Nazi invasion of Poland, led the uprising in the Vilna ghetto bringing the survivors to safety through the sewers and then the forests. Perhaps it was his voice in the back of my car as I drove him to his friend's apartment. Kovner said: "What does a poet do with such a biography? He swaddles the words and rocks them in his lap like a mother does to a child. Don't cry, words, don't cry."

The continuity of the language can be felt in two love poems, one Biblical, one contemporary. From the "Song of Songs":

Rise up, my love, my fair one, and come way
for lo, the winter is past
The rain is over and gone:
The flowers appear on the earth;
The time of singing is come
And the voice of the turtle is heard in our land.

Come, my beloved, let us go forth into the field . . .

Let us see whether the vine hath budded
whether the vine-blossom be opened
And the pomegranates be in flower.

The second, by Israeli poet T. Carmi, bears a close relationship to the first. Carmi, whose name was Carmi Charny, was born in America. He did not spend his summer holidays in camps. His father used to rent a bungalow in the mountains where he gave Carmi a daily two-hour Bible lesson and a nickel reward for each chapter Carmi mastered. Carmi tells us that "it all became part of me and still is and this must be why I did my first writing in Hebrew." He went to France as a teacher for the Jewish war orphans in the summer of 1946. After a year he returned to New York where he received a scholarship from the Zionist Organization of America to study at the Hebrew University. In the interview he was asked: Are you ready to come back and contribute to the life of the American Jewish community? Yes, he lied, without compunction. He arrived in Israel in October 1947, studied for six weeks at Mount Scopus, joined the Haganah and fought in the War of Liberation. His poem, "To the Pomegranate," goes this way:

> Go away, go away from here
> Go to other eyes.
> I already wrote about you yesterday.
>
> I said green
> To your branches bowing in the wind
> And red red red
> To the drops of your fruit.
> I cried light to your root
> The moist and dark and stubborn.
>
> Now you do not exist.
> Now you block my view of the day
> And the moon that hasn't yet risen.
>
> Come!
> I wrote about you the day before yesterday
>
> And your young memory
> Stings my hands like nettle.
> Come and see the strange pomegranate:
> Its blood is in my veins, on my head in my hands
> And still it is emplanted in its place.[6]

As for the lessons, as for my learning Hebrew, it is not yet finished. Have I learned the language finally? Can I open the Siddur or the book of poetry or turn to the newspaper and read? Can I speak aloud in the tongue of my forefathers? And understand what is spoken to me?

The story is not over yet. But once, when I was sleeping in Jerusalem between the Dead Sea and the Mount of Olives, I dreamed that the patriarchs came into my room. They were dressed in flowing blue robes covered with gold like the wrapping and mantle that cover the Torah, and they spoke to me in that ancient language, and I knew what they said and I answered them.

WHO HAS NOT DREAMED

OF FLYING?

I was once in an elevator face-to-face with Isaac Bashevis Singer.
He had just given a talk on why it was not necessary to create
any more characters for our fiction. God the novelist, he told us,
had made more than enough characters to go around! I over-
came for once my difficulty in speaking and said to him: Your
talk reminds me of Aaron Zeitlin's poem about how we are all
of us illustrations to the text—"stones, people, little shards of
glass in the sun . . . the pictures fall off like shriveled parts." Ah,
Zeitlin, Singer exclaimed. Before I die I want to translate
Zeitlin's poetry. He was the best of the Yiddish poets, Singer told
me. Suddenly the elevator made that tiny adjustment, matching
floor to floor, the door opened, and the Yiddish air inside evap-
orated. Now we were in a hallway of a government building,
ordinary people once more.

Who has not dreamed of flying? Yasha, Singer's magician of
Lublin, lying in the bed of his mistress wonders "why he had not
tried it before—it was so easy, so easy . . . If a bird could do it,
why not man? Man was heavier than a bird, but eagles and
hawks were not exactly light either, and they could even lift a

lamb and fly away with it. Simply let the material be strong enough, the ribs elastic, the man agile, light and sprightly, and the deed must be accomplished. What a sensation it would cause throughout the world if he, Yasha, flew over the rooftops of Warsaw or better still—Rome, or London."

Hesitating Bird by Lithuanian artist Adomas Jacovskis.

Isaac Bashevis Singer has met his magician's specifications: the material is strong enough, the ribs elastic, the man agile, and the deed continues to be accomplished. His stories—which come from vanished dots on the map of Jewish Poland—fly up over the rooftops of Warsaw, of Rome, Paris, and London. They have even crossed the Atlantic and come to us here.

In the Greek myth, the boy Icarus flies too close to the sun. His error is full of grandeur; he is immortalized by artists and writers from Ovid and Brueghel to those of our century. In Singer's stories the flight is noisy; the flyer is barely aloft. There are few heroics, and no heroes. Yasha's dream of flying occurs in a bed just off the kitchen. That bed, like an appendage, like a *shtetl*, is only inches away from others.

Just as the stories fly, so are they weighted—wedded to this earth—by the matter of which they are composed. Still thinking of his dream of flying when Magda comes into the bed, Yasha runs his hand down her emaciated ribs and asks: "What's the matter with you? Don't you eat?" "Yes," she answers him, "I eat." "It would be easy for you to fly," he tells her. "You weigh about as much as a goose." And later, the smallest tremor of flight: "He embraced her and she fluttered like a pullet in his arms."

Even in speech, Singer's nouns and verbs fly. Yasha has ended his holiday stay with his wife and sets off for a series of visits that will lead him back to his ultimate love, Emilia. On the way, he stops off at Zeftel's house where he must listen to her complaints before making love. "Even as she complained, the words shot out—smooth and round, like peas from a peashooter."

Yasha, the magician of Lublin, has access to all things. Those who are cautious even about crossing the border of a single street are amazed by this one who is able to bypass the prohibitions of the Jews, of Gentiles. He is not confined to place, to one woman, to one God. He can walk a tightrope, skate on a wire, climb walls. With a shoemaker's awl or a simple wire Yasha can unlock any safe, open any door. There is no obstacle which Yasha cannot overcome.

Passage between the visible and the nonvisible world is a matter that Singer's characters negotiate with ease. In the pages depicting these worlds, Singer has filled in every available space. Only his design is not that of an artist who has a terror of emptiness, like the early Greek potters whose creations are filled with geometric designs devoid of grace. It is more the design of the Creator who has sought to bring to life each sleeping letter, each small stone and grain of sand. The world, in Singer's hands, is transformed and illuminated and animated by the past, by the Torah and Talmud, by Midrash, by the lives of those who dwell in this world, by the imagined lives of those who have never been born, by those who were here once and are no longer among us. All come to life in his hands, in the patient carving out—as in *The Slave,* Jacob carving on a stone behind the barn with a small bent hook the words of the commandments, the words of Torah he was recreating from memory and out of the very tissue of his life.

But in flight is the certainty of fall; the daydreams sent upward fall back upon us. The world animated by living things, that same world which Jacob describes as a "parchment scrawled with words and song," can just as suddenly contain fantasies that cannot be driven off: "He ridiculed his fancies but could not banish them. Like locusts they fell upon him; daydreams of harem girls, slaves; tricks that were beyond nature; magic potions, charms and incantations that unfolded all secrets and bestowed infinite powers."

And that which falls to us has a mind of its own: "Jacob stood in front of the granary and watched the snow falling. Some of the flakes dropped straight to earth and others swirling and eddied as if seeking to return to the heavenly storehouses."

And flight separates us. Following the Chmielnicki massacres, a survivor tells Jacob and Sarah: "I was already in the other world and I saw my mother. There was music and I didn't walk but floated like a bird. My mother flew beside me. We came to two mountains with a pass between. The pass was as red as sunset and smelled of the spices of Paradise. My mother skimmed through but when I tried to follow someone drove me back. I opened my eyes and someone was dragging me. I was being pulled from the cellar by a Cossack. I begged him to kill me but those who want to die live." The Jew no longer had access, not to the churches of the Christians, not even to what was familiar in himself. Driven off, dragged through the streets, chained to horses or left to wander in the forests, the Jew had become earthbound.

Singer's world is unredeemed by the piety of its inhabitants. It is a satanic, primitive world where people behave inexplicably, where faith brings not redemption but downfall. *The Magician of Lublin* closes with Yasha inexplicably locked into a tower of his own making, cut off from the world he had maneuvered so expertly, with such ease. He becomes an ascetic who has deliberately chosen to be locked into the cold and isolation. Is this a joke? Is he parodying the medieval ascetics? Why do his antics, his flight, something we rejoiced over, something we exalted in,

something we longed for ourselves, come to this? Or does his end sig-
nify that the options we are each given—a life, a God if we can believe
in Him, love if we are capable of it—are limited, perhaps not real
options after all.

During the Days of Awe the following tale is often recounted: When
Abraham lifted up his eyes at Mount Moriah he beheld a ram caught in
the thicket by his horns. Did the ram, tearing himself free from one
thicket, only become entangled in another, just as man is destined to be
caught in iniquity and entangled in misfortune?

The question is not answered but the parable goes on: No part of
the ram went to waste. Its ashes became the base of the inner altar. The
sinews were torn corresponding to the ten strings of the harp of David,
its skin became the girdle of Elijah's loins, the voice of the left horn was
heard on Mount Sinai, the right to be blown at the ingathering of the
dispersed.

The images of Singer, the world of the *shtetl*, fly down to us, noth-
ing wasted, as with the ram of Abraham. Each rooster in the barnyard,
each toad and pullet of the world, all used, all transformed, carried
through Singer to us.

It was never a work for the critics, not for the rabbis and the pious.
But in that work as in no other, the *shtetl*, the lives and dreams of those
who died, will fly over the rooftops of time, and later on when those who
live look up into the pages of Isaac Bashevis Singer's stories, they will
find the pullets and geese, the ordinary men and women of that vanished
world having their extraordinary dreams. And every corner of their
homely, impoverished and infinitely rich world will be illuminated by
what he has imagined.[7]

YIDDISH POETRY

The particular, so absorbing to the Yosemite climber, his hammock suspended from pitons over empty space, is reminiscent of Yiddish suspended between the dot under the letter Yud, the smallest vowel sign of the smallest letter in the Hebrew alphabet, which nonetheless begins the tetragrammaton YHVH for the name of God. And like the covenant at Sinai in which all—even those not yet born—participated, Yiddish, a language in use for over a thousand years, has produced a unique literature that adds a strong link in the history and culture of the Jewish people.

Like the *Bovo-Buch*, a verse epic of the adventures of Prince Bovo composed by Elijah Levita in 1507, and the *Shmuel-Buch*, an heroic epic with a Jewish hero, the *Penguin Book of Yiddish Poetry* provides powerful evidence of this culture. That there were between ten and twelve million Yiddish-speaking people at the outbreak of World War II and a far smaller number at this writing, makes this collection of poetry all the more precious. Some of the poets have been presented in earlier works: Howe and Greenberg's fine collection, *A Treasury of Yiddish Poetry*; Ruth Whitman's *Yiddish Poetry*, the Jewish Publication Society's individual collections, and a number of anthologies. In this bilingual work—I cannot stress enough the importance of having the Yiddish original: one can see, study, and compare even without a great knowledge of the original—six poets are presented in depth, chosen as the "strongest, the most characteristic, and the most accessible in translation." So we find Moyshe-Leyb Halpern—original, colloquial, Biblical, his poetry an influence for Manger and Glatstein. In a poem on the death of Peretz he writes: "And you're dead. And you've not yet been covered by the ground/ . . . And everyone with a tongue/ Inside his head now beats out, like a shoemaker's young/ Apprentice, hammering away at a heavy nail/ In an old shoe's heel, pounds out a rhythmic dirge, a wail. Every sound is full of dirt . . ." The poem contains the plaint of a Job, and is an antiphonal counterpoint to the Kaddish.

Here is Itsik Manger, "folk bard"; Moyshe Kulbak who wrote about old-country village life and cosmopolitan deracination in the Europe of 1920; Perets Markish, the great Soviet Yiddish expressionist poet; Jacob Glatstein, who brought the modernist impulse into Yiddish poetry; and Abraham Sutzkever, whose journey from Siberia to Vilna to Israel embodies a central line of modern Jewish experience. Sutzkever, the only one of the six alive today, is the editor of *Di Goldene Keyt,* the leading Yiddish literary journal in Israel, and is a master poet, author of numerous books. In addition to works by these six, there are selections of the works of thirty-three others.

Abraham Sutzkever says in his introduction to this collection that Yiddish poetry "is a poetry of homelessness and dislocation . . . One of its functions is to cast about, directly or obliquely, for new surrogate homes."

Sutzkever goes on to say: "The idea of a self-sufficient secular Yiddish culture, wedged between the overpowering presences of the Hebraic past and the Western present, proves to be inherently fragile . . . . The closer a secular Yiddish culture comes to achieving its fulfillment, the closer it comes to preparing its own destruction." This passage and all its dangers is the subject of much of the poetry. As is the effort to speak to God on new terms following the Holocaust. Witness the narrator in Jacob Glatstein's poem, "Genesis":

Why don't we start all over again
With a small people,
out of the cradle and little?

. . .

Almighty Yahweh, who has waxed great
over the seven firmaments and continents,
swollen steel-strong in vast churches
and synagogues, God of the Universe,
You've deserted field and barn:

. . .

We followed You into Your wide world
and sickened there.
Save Yourself, return
with Your pilgrims who go up
to a little land. Come back,
be our Jewish God again.[8]

translated by Cynthia Ozick

Sutzkever's childhood commenced in Siberia where his parents fled during the World War I. Later he was a member of the literary artistic group Yung Vilna in the 1930s and became a forceful presence in the Vilna Ghetto. In 1943 he escaped to the partisans and then to Moscow. After the war he testified at the Nuremberg trials, spent time in Lodz, Paris, and in 1947, came to Israel. "In the Sack of the Wind," written in 1935, records the spiritual journey and strangely forecasts events to come:

A barefoot vagabond on a stone
in evening's gold
shakes off
the dust of the world.
Suddenly, from out of the woods
a bird flies
and snatches up the last grain of sun.

. . .

What is there to do at such a moment.
O my world of a thousand colors,
but to gather up that beautiful redness
in the sack of the wind
and bring it home for supper.

And then there's loneliness, like a mountain.

translated by Chana Bloch

And the poem "How?" written in the Vilna Ghetto, February 14, 1943:

> How will you fill your goblet
> On the day of liberation? And with what?
> Are you prepared, in your joy, to endure
> The dark keening you have heard
> Where skulls of day glitter
> In a bottomless pit?
>
> You will search for a key to fit
> Your jammed locks. You will bite
> The sidewalks like bread,
> Thinking: It used to be better.
> And time will gnaw at you like a cricket
> Caught in a fist.
>
> Then your memory will resemble
> An ancient buried town.
> And your estranged eyes will burrow
> Like a mole, a mole . . .
>
> *translated by Chana Bloch*

In this powerful collection of Yiddish poetry, every part of Jewish learning is present, from Torah to Talmud to Midrash, and blended here are the lands and peoples encountered by the poets in their wandering. Unlike our Yosemite climber, nailed to the enormous vertical desert of the cliff face, our poets reside in the horizontal, the stream of light we call time, which binds us to the past and carries the covenants established there, through poetry, to this day.

MOROCCO

Gauze Curtains, Round Tombs, Hidden Jews

*I*n Marrakesh—a great African trading center at the edge of the Sahara—I walk to the synagogue for Shabbat service. I think about the journeys of Jews through strange lands as I hear the biblical portion about Joseph in Egypt. In Casablanca—once a French colonial town—as we women sit in the Lubavitcher synagogue, separated from the men by glass doors and a gauze curtain, the portion read aloud is the Song of Deborah, perhaps the only truly liberated female in the Bible.

In the Marrakesh cemetery, I walk along a shaded road and become aware of women begging at the gate. Some I had seen the day before at the home for the aged. Amir Haloum presses a coin into the folded bony fingers of a man lying on the ground in semisleep.

I pass through an opening between tall trees, and in the bright morning light it is as though I have come upon several eras of our history. I remember the original twelve tribes and think how our people were scattered upon the face of the earth like the remnants of a great star.

The graves go in all directions like letters in an alphabet mysteriously obliterated by age; the tombs, like raised letters, spell out their stories across the face of the field. The language cannot any longer be read. But the story continues.

I walk over to the new section. The rounded tombs are made of concrete and bits of stone, with no inscriptions, but each with a small recess in which to place a candle. Who will remember the names of those who are buried here? I ask myself. No one answers.

Morocco—as beautiful a face as was given to earth. Folded mountains and great canyons. River valleys and oases. Broad reaches of desert, colored sienna. Snow-covered mountains, cedar forests. And peopled with ancient tribes who speak in the tongues of each of the three sons of Noah: Berbers who use a Hamitic language; Jews and Arabs, their Semitic dialects; French and Spanish—languages of Japhet—are used everywhere.

Among the stones of the river valleys, the women wash their hand-woven robes—blue, red and striped. Or they stand along an escarpment, cloaked in layers of garments, their dark hair braided. Looking up at them, one wonders if they are part of a world that is not yet visible to us. Or if they are shadows from a world that no longer exists.

As a woman leans to cover her face with her blue robe, so are the doors and walls veiled from our eyes by shadows. In the dim light, through a small opening in a doorway, I see great amphoras leaning, as they must have leaned for centuries, against the earthen walls. Amphoras like those from the days before the exile in Babylonia, before the First Temple was completed.

From Ouarzazate—where civilians have been armed against the Polisario guerrillas roaming the desert roads at night—I pass through the oasis of Skoura, which once had seven Jewish quarters, where roses are cultivated and where there are sugar plantations. I visit Tiliit, part of the only foreign Jewish group ever to have come to the Tiliit *mellah*— the Jewish quarter said to be older than that of Marrakesh. The name of the local Berber tribe is Iouartiguine.

We are presented to a tall, imposing-looking man wearing a striped white-and–grayish brown jellaba and white turban. His name is Ha-sanin M'Barak Ouharron. He surprises us by reciting in Hebrew the blessing over the wine and another one for the slaughter of cows. "When they left their homes they kissed the *mezuzot* on the doorposts of their houses," he tells us, referring to the Jews who once lived there. "And where have they gone?" one of us asks him. "Only God knows what has become of them," he responds. "I myself do not know my own origin."

We are invited to his home. We are seated in the traditional way, on benches hugging the four walls. Sweet mint tea is brought in small glasses. Almonds are passed on white ceramic plates. He welcomes us in Hebrew, making the blessing over the tea. He sings Shabbat *zmirot*.

"When the Jews left," he says, "we embraced and cried. We lived and worked together for tens of years. If a Muslim needed a loan it would be done by word, without a written contract. They were like our brothers." What work did the Jews do, he is asked. "They dealt in livestock, olive oil, sugar."

M'Barak walks with us to the cemetery. Children and other villagers follow us. The tombs are made of earth and stones, mounds full of small boulders and pebbles. He tells us that he used to be responsible for the care of the cemetery, that he would safeguard the belongings of the dead until the family came to claim them.

It is difficult to distinguish the graves from the earth. A man walking beside me points to the ground in front of me. Here is a grave of a child—the pebbles and stone are arranged in an oval shape smaller than the others.

"How many Jews are buried here?" M'Barak is asked. "How many liters of water are there in the sea?" he answers. He recites a psalm of David in Hebrew.

A young woman said to be his daughter discovers that one in our group is named Esther. Perhaps because this is also her name or perhaps because it is the name of someone who once lived in her village or perhaps for a reason we shall never know, she reaches out to embrace our Esther and parades her through the village, repeating her name aloud.

M'Barak bids us farewell in Hebrew. I find in my hand a small white wax candle and a shard from a tomb.

It has been written, usually in the past tense, that in remote Moroccan villages there were old and venerable rabbis with a profound knowledge of Torah, which they knew by heart, and of the Talmud, which they studied and taught, and of the Cabala, whose mysteries they meditated upon, and that they possessed a spiritual purity and a simplicity of manner. Such a man is Mordechai Ben Moshe Sebbagh of Erfoud. Blind, in his eighties, he lives with his elderly and ailing wife Mennoch Mamene and daughter Mizel, who cares for them. We visit with him in a room barely furnished and uncomfortably cold. He wears a beige caftan and has a long white beard and thick white eyebrows. He speaks in Hebrew of the 1,600 Jews who once lived in Erfoud, of the seven synagogues that once were. He tells us that his family came from Rissani—where the remains of a synagogue we visited were inhabited by a donkey tethered to the *bima*.

Mizel wears a printed dress and kerchief. Her black hair is gathered into several long braids, twisted and looped. When we ask to take her picture she stands stiffly at her father's side. Her animated face becomes expressionless before the camera.

When we leave, we are reminded of the observance of Tevet, the fast day that commemorates the siege of Jerusalem by Nebuchadnezzar, King of Babylon. As it is said in Kings: "On the ninth day of the fourth month the famine was sore in the city, so that there was no bread for the people of the land. Then a breach was made in the city, and all the men of war fled by night by way of the gate between the two walls, which was by the king's garden—now the Chaldeans were against the city round about. . . . And they slew the sons of Zedekiah before his eyes, and put out the eyes of Zedekiah, and bound him in fetters, and carried him to Babylon."

Errachidia—also known as Ksar es Souk or the Fortified Village of the Market—is an ancient village, half of which was once inhabited by Jews. Its Jewish community is known to date at least as far back as Roman times. In 1955 there were 830 Jews here; fifteen years ago, 300. Now there are four remaining families—a total of nineteen souls. Of the three synagogues, two are in disrepair. One synagogue is named for Rabbi Shimon Bar Yochai, author of the Zohar. Each is a typical Sephardi structure with four columns, and the bima in the center. When there is no *minyan,* prayers are recited individually.

Chetrit is the name of the leading family. Joseph Chetrit is a tailor; his wife Yacout is the president of the community. All but the youngest of their children live elsewhere: two daughters in Casablanca; another daughter in Paris; a married daughter in Afula, Israel. A son in Geneva is studying engineering.

Madame Chetrit takes us to the cemetery, and we visit the tomb of Rabbi Yechiah Laulou. She has seen to the renovation of the tomb and the pavilion over it. The money—3,500 dirham (about $800)—came from Israel and other countries.

We are handed candles to light and to place in the recesses of the tomb—a custom strange to American Jews. The veneration of *tzaddikim* (righteous) is peculiarly North African. Some of them are honored throughout the country; there are others whose fame is confined to a particular region. Most villages have their local saints and frequently they are venerated by Muslim and Jew alike. One scholarly study has revealed the existence of thirty-one saints claimed by both Jew and Muslim. One unusual example is Solica in the Jewish Cemetery of Fez. She was seventeen when she refused to join the king's harem or to accept Islam. Her suicide in 1834 symbolized Jewish resistance, yet to this day she is venerated by Muslims who rarely accord such status to women.

At Rabbi Laulou's tomb, Madame Chetrit says that we may make three wishes—and the tomb has three recesses for candles. She tells us that the most common wishes are for marriage and fertility.

As she takes us through the *mellah* where she was raised, Madame Chetrit reprimands the government official who accompanies us, because a disused synagogue has been boarded up. She extracts a promise that nothing more will be changed in the building and that no one will be allowed to live there.

Like other Moroccan Jews, she is careful not to mention the word *Israel,* but refers instead to the *pays*—the country. In schools, when Hebrew melodies are sung, "lalala" is substituted for the word *Israel.* But children do not hesitate to recite the word *Israel* when it is part of material they are learning. The rules here are subtle and complex.

Madame Chetrit tells of the close relationships between Jews and Berbers. In the old days, during times of tribal warfare, Jews would send their wives and children to Berber families for safety. We learn that nowadays many of the men of the Berber tribes work in France as laborers.

Madame Chetrit was one of the first to volunteer to take part in the Green March of 1975—the famous demonstration in which one million Moroccans marched into Spanish Sahara to dramatize the country's claim to the land evacuated by Spain.

She tells us that in the old days, girls married at thirteen or fourteen; now at around twenty. As the Jewish communities have dwindled, particularly in villages on the fringes of the Sahara, it has become more difficult to find mates.

If Casablanca is Morocco's New York and Rabat, its Washington, Fez is its Jerusalem, nestled in a valley and covered with mist. The mountains hover over, and the morning's light and mist suggest a veil.

Fez was a great center of Jewish learning. The sage who is the symbol of Hebrew scholarship in North Africa was Rabbi Isaac ben Jacob Alfassi (1013–1103), a native of Fez who drew up a compendium of the Talmud. Fez is where Moses Maimonides—Rambam—studied for several years. When we ask about setting up some sort of memorial in the house where his family lived, we are told that it might provide a focus for vandalism. Others say that there are plans for a commemorative plaque. Still others contend that the Jewish community has never requested a memorial.

Here and there we hear whispers that the government has confiscated some Jewish properties and that certain jobs are closed to Jews. There are moments when a person talking with us about difficulties is urged by others to keep quiet. When we ask people in high positions, we get different answers. About confiscation, we are told that those wishing to go abroad often arrange to do so without losing all their worldly goods, and attempt to do so without paying up taxes. On the other hand, transfers of property admittedly take many years, unless one is well-placed or has high connections. The bureaucratic structure involves long delays.

We hear that when the law on Jerusalem was voted by the Knesset last July, the Moroccan news media conducted a sustained anti-Israel attack that had its effect on the Jews. But King Hassan's concern with the Jewish community is undeniable. For instance, the governor of Casablanca—the city and province where the majority of Morocco's 20,000 Jews lives—traditionally attends Rosh Hashana or Yom Kippur services at the leading synagogue. Last year, the governor happened to be out of the country, as was his deputy. No representation would have been seen by the Jews as signaling a withdrawal of the royal protection at a time when some Jews were fearful of going to Yom Kippur services. When this was pointed out, King Hassan instructed a member of the cabinet to go to the synagogue, and the event was featured on Moroccan television.

One influential Moroccan Jew muses: "Look there are twenty million Muslims in this country and there cannot be a policeman behind each one. Though King Hassan shields us, he would not be able to prevent a stone being thrown against a shop or stop a fanatic crowd. But if the day comes when I must pray with the windows and doors of the synagogue locked, I too will not be able to remain." Referring to the tens of thousands of Jews who emigrated after Morocco's independence in 1956, he says: "Those who left have left us both the Torah and their debts. We must assume both."

WHAT HASANIN M'BARAK SAID

If you ask
how many are buried here,
I must ask you how many liters
of water are in the sea.

At their doorposts they kept
nailed a passage
in strange script which
they touched
with their fingers
and brought to their lips
whenever they entered.

They taught us
to say this blessing
over bread and this
over wine and this for the slaughter
of animals.

And why did you not recite
the blessing yourself
over the tea just then?

When they left us
we embraced them like brothers
for they had given us pleasure
as we had them.

We have taken their names
for our children.
When we call our sons,
our daughters, we carry
in our voices
a small song of their names.

We do not know
what became of them.
Have you seen them
on your way in
to this place?

Like a Field Riddled
by Ants

In the Afterlife Which

Is a Library

*I*n the afterlife which is a library I am in the stacks when one of
my 413 sins walks up to me: Why didn't you answer my letter?
it asks. What is your name? I say, looking at it curiously. We
have paused near the Rashi commentaries. We obviously are
both after the same thing.

I think to myself, I knew it wasn't good when my analyst
told me to forget about guilt. But what, I had argued with him,
should I do about the 613 good deeds I hadn't yet performed?
He leaned back in his Viennese chair among the figurines he was
always collecting. Sometimes I couldn't see his face for all the
wood and soapstone, all the little fertility figures, the male
house idols, the nubile girls. I couldn't think sometimes, it was
so distracting.

He leaned back. All this talk, all my money, and nothing
comes to take away this terrible ache. If I could fill up the
empty places with words, I would. But it doesn't work. I don't
mention this to him though. I don't think he would under-
stand. It's the same with hunger: it's hard to fill up on preposi-
tions and adverbs.

So there he is, leaning back in his chair. I can see the whites of his legs where his socks don't quite meet the bottom of his trousers. I am distracted again. Meanwhile I am talking about Charles Darwin and his beloved barnacles, about the return of the Monarch butterfly to West Virginia. And he is asking me what I think the conflict is really about. And I am imagining I am in the backseat of a car with a boy who is seventeen and I am seventeen.

He is leaning back in his chair when your face comes around the corner again. He clears his throat waiting for me to speak and I feel guilty. All that money going by like minutes and nothing said. Still the silence. He leans back, waiting. I try to open my mouth but each time I do, I find your face pressed against mine. He gives up waiting and starts to talk. What thoughts do you have about this silence? he ventures. Suddenly I am sitting on the front stoop in full moonlight with you. I am breathing in the cool spring air.

Meanwhile, back in the stacks I meet up with this fellow. I knew, I just knew it would be like this. They would all be waiting for me, waiting their turns. And he is there, holding out all the letters he ever wrote to me, demanding to know why I stopped writing to him. What could I say? What would you have said?

Another of my sins comes along: I sent you my manuscript, my life's work, and you never wrote to me. You never even read it. In a black bound journal, which he is waving around in my face, I can see the bloodstains, the salty residue of tears, the concentric circles like tree rings of spilled coffee, his lifework poured out. And I have ignored him, have been unresponsive. But the worst, the absolute worst is the young girl who stands shyly and accusingly in the corner. It was my birthday, she whispers to me, my sixteenth birthday and I wrote to you and I sent you my poems and you never answered my letter. You never sent me a critique of my thirty-seven poems. What could I say? What would you have said? I pressed in among the books hoping I could avoid the eyes of the rest of them. Suddenly someone came running down the aisle: You let the policy lapse, he was shouting at me. You didn't make the payments.

I crouch down beside Rabbi Nahman of Bratzlav. I lean down next to Rabbi Akiba, the gentle martyr who is still wrapped in the parchment scrolls of the Torah. It is true they are singed by the fire the Romans put to him years ago, but the letters are all intact. What do you have to say, Master? I whisper to Akiba. What can you advise me? I say urgently. But his reply is a terrible silence. I press in against Moses and Abraham. But I am not hidden from sight.

THE MESSENGER

*S*ometimes I believe they are sent to me. God's messengers. To test me. This one never smiled. He stood in the doorway of my office, solid as a tree trunk. The confusion of phones ringing, conversations of colleagues, urgent students, never fazed him. He was his grandmother's emissary.

Which century had he come from? His dark hair was painted onto his head like the Golem's. He stared at me as though I should recognize him. "You wrote the story about Singer," he announced. And then he told me his name. Surely I had never met him before. In fact, I had never seen anyone who looked like him. Thick glasses. Inside them, his eyes floated like carp. I didn't know which one to focus on.

He was clutching a thick manilla envelope, the kind with a red string wound several times around the circular clasp. I offered him a chair. "My grandmother . . ." he began. I knew before he finished the sentence. I was to be the literary agent for his grandmother who had spent seven years writing this story. Well, actually it was a novel. The package contained a summary and outline of the chapters and a letter from his grandmother as well as a few sample chapters. I was to find a publisher for his grandmother, arrange the best deal.

He short thick arms kept making gestures like speech that can't quite leave the throat of its speaker, quick jabs. Arms, moving toward me and away, with that manuscript. I made no move to relieve him of his burden. I remembered a story about Alexander Pope who kept his arms folded behind his back on such occasions so that he would not appear to invite the flock of pages. But a grandmother. And this boy. An emissary in the long family of emissaries. She had written a novel that started with the Bible and spanned three millennia. And here was I, the sacred recipient, with my hands tightly clenched behind my back.

My office mate interrupted her conversation with a student to slyly watch me. But she never said a word to me about it afterward. I knew she wondered how I would handle this one. There had been others. Many others over the years.

The grandmother's novel started in Biblical times, traveled through the Babylonian exile to the Roman period, continued to the Crusades, took in dozens of massacres, pogroms, mass suicides, heroic acts, false messiahs, cabalistic rituals, lingered for quite a time at the Holocaust as though not knowing how to surmount that place for the ashes were still rising from the chimneys, and then spread out among the valleys and hills of Israel where it seemed to fuse with the landscape. Somehow it managed to separate itself once again, until it rapped soundly upon the door of the last quarter of the twentieth century. It was all there, he assured me, in the package he still tried to shove toward me.

By now, my office chair had rolled into the filing cabinet. Soon I would be near the window. I watched a pigeon making his escape from a window across the parking lot. He was clumsy in his hideous red galoshes. I envied him. I would have done anything at that moment to escape the scrutiny of my messenger. The boy was so serious, so earnest. He never smiled. He seemed to be taking a reading of my face, each eye deciding for itself. But whatever conclusion he came to, I could not fathom it.

Once, after I had given a talk in a synagogue an old Russian woman named Karamazov invited me to come home with her to live. But first she poured me a cup of tea, fed me three or four cakes, insisted that no one speak to me until I had eaten. She too was a messenger. I knew I must be careful, make no mistake. These messengers were like the Thirty-six Just, the hearts of the world multiplied, who take upon themselves the suffering of all. It is said that when an unknown Just rises to heaven, God must warm him for a thousand years in his fingers, so frozen is he by the sorrows of this world. Without them, none of the rest of us would be alive.

But I said no to Mrs. Karamazov. I said goodbye to Mrs. Karamazov. And I never understood why I said no. I could feel the messenger recede, my opportunity disappear. I had failed a test whose purpose no one had ever bothered to explain to me.

What could he be thinking? Had he sprung whole cloth from an egg? From the hatchery or the sea? Who was he? Who had sent him to me that afternoon? He had only hesitated briefly at my door. He seemed to know me instinctively, seeking out my face as he pronounced my name. I felt outnumbered by him though I was taller, older. He seemed immovable, like a boulder, like a fire hydrant. He hadn't called to make an appointment. Yet he'd found me in.

"I haven't an agent myself," I heard myself telling him. "I haven't even a publisher," I said plaintively, hoping he'd pity me. "And I don't know anything about novels," I said firmly. This time my chair had wedged itself against the radiator. I felt like I was on fire.

An inspiration: I began pulling open the drawer of the metal filing cabinet. I'd give him a list of agents. I'd find him the name of an editor who had published my article. Let someone else deal with his grandmother. I'd suffer whatever punishment clearly was in store for me. He didn't move a muscle. He didn't flinch. He didn't change his expression. I watched him as I flurried through the papers in the file cabinet. I opened drawer after drawer, one yellow folder, one green. No luck. Finally I came to the brown paper with an address on it. "Here," I said. "Copy down this address. Give it to your grandmother. No, on second thought, give the whole pamphlet to her. Let her keep it." And I spelled out the name of the editor.

He watched me, somehow unconvinced. He was on another track. Nothing I could do would derail him. "My grandmother," he continued as though his sentence had calmly started years ago, "would like it if you could read her novel and write her a note afterward telling her what you think of it. It would be very important to her."

"January," I muttered, "nothing to read until January," I stuttered, the words coming out wrong, as though January were a soggy log floating in the sea that I had just grabbed ahold of rather than permit myself to drown. "This is the end of the semester," I heard myself tell him. "See these papers?" I threw them up into the air, a whole set of student papers to convince him. He never batted an eyelash. "I have to read all of this first. Besides, I haven't anything to say to a novelist. It wouldn't be of any special use to your grandmother, what I might think of her book."

He rose, he rose in his chair like a battalion of sturdy soldiers, they all ascended with him. The packet still in his hand, he turned away from me and walked slowly, slowly to the door and he never looked back. The place where he had been, that place above the threshold, seemed to retain his shape for a long time afterward.

He is gone now. I do not see him clearly in my mind's eye. But that packet in his hand, those pages that I never asked him to hand to me, the story whose beginning I shall never see—how it burns there in my mind, how it stares at me. How curious I have grown to see how it all began, the letters moving together to make words, the words settling down alongside one another into sentences, the sentences telling their story. For days I have tried to imagine what that old woman could have written, what that solemn boy held in his hands that day. Messenger, emissary, shape in my doorway: Tell me what it was she wrote.

GETTING THERE

*A*aron and Joseph, as the sisters were called—their mother had taken quite literally the injunction to name after the dead— struggled to find the route to the cemetery. One drove, the other navigated. When they were sufficiently lost, they reversed roles.

There was a ritual uncertainty about getting to the cemetery. Charts and maps were prepared beforehand. Bridges were accounted for; alternate routes studied and rehearsed. But even as they drove, the road stretched out before them, increasing itself to the horizon; their small green car appeared to be making no headway at all. Joseph would cheerfully call out the route names and landmarks, sanctifying each with her voice, enveloping them as if she were wrapping Chinese pastries.

But nothing helped. How many times they had come to bury members of their family. To unveil headstones. To plant on the graves. The sisters would drive bravely through the day, plotting their course, adjusting the route to account for the mysterious streets that flung themselves helter-skelter like barricades along their passage.

The first tombstones rose up like living matter, fitful and silent in the distance. What they had been avoiding during the long drive loomed before them now. But what was it? The fact of the bones floating in the wooden boxes, the flesh seeping away through two holes in the bottom of the coffin? Or the hands of the Kohanim carved into the tombstones, the paired fingers pointing stiffly like the horns of a ram, making the priestly benediction? All those hands, loosened from their owners, more accusation than blessing? Or the souls who wandered ceaselessly in the graveyard, stripped of their husks of speech? No word to divert them. Their space in the world unoccupied.

Or was it the thought of their own deaths they had wished to avoid? The territory between themselves and these souls seemed discontinuous, a place they couldn't negotiate. The two sisters had come this far. But the rest of the journey?

Like the dividing line that separated portions of time. Like that instant when the millennium would turn and nineteen hundred ninety-nine years would simply fall back into the sleep of years.

Some equated this event with total annihilation. Others saw nothing spectacular about it. Some skipped over the present and rushed headlong into the future. Others lagged behind. And some hid under a bush.

But the two sisters, Joseph and Aaron, were looking backward together. Which gave them both the illusion of looking ahead, of reading things to come. Aaron had wondered when her mother left them one cold February morning where she was going next. She had carried her mother in her small basket of skin up to the edge of the welcoming glass, but who, she had asked, would pour her like wine to its vessel? Who would take her the rest of the way? How would the heritage go on?

With her heel braced against the lip of the sharp metal shovel, Aaron set her weight against the earth, pitching this way and that until a clump of clay and grass gave way. Those who had come to pray were disturbed by the work of the sisters. Several, interrupting their prayers, went to the caretaker's house to report them. The pious swayed and bent their knees. They prayed above the dead like dark angels. Their Cadillacs shone patent leather black in the September sun. The attack dogs strained on their leashes and the alarm system sent up a wall of sound even Joshua couldn't have brought down. The sisters transported green hoses, turned on faucets, measured out root hormone, fertilizer, and moist humus. They dug into the graves as if they meant to disinter their parents.

The prayers of the pious rose up into the trees, opening and closing their wings as if they planned to roost there for all of eternity. There was about this season a heightened urgency to mend one's fences, to repent, to visit the neglected dead. The small pebbles left by the visitors on the graves pulled themselves into letters. Some spelled out secret messages from the living. Others carried the sleeping words of those buried beneath the stones—warnings and forecasts. Complaints.

There were more arguments in this season than usual. And more reconciliations. The prayers twittered in the trees, giving off those last chattering songs before they grew silent.

The sisters took pains not to disturb Crankshaw's grave. Some Crankshaw descendant was bound to turn up, to become indignant at the sight of tan bark and humus sliding down toward Crankshaw's space, even if the magnolia tree would someday provide shade for all of them. Perhaps a succulent blossom would fall upon Crankshaw's portion, close enough to his grave for him to inhale the lemon odor and remember the world.

They were kneeling in the ditch they had created above their parents, the humus floating like an enormous black planet in the pool of water where it had not yet been mixed with soil, when they caught sight of two brown shoes. Joseph tilted her head upward, taking in a pair of checkered trousers, a flannel shirt, and, above that, a furious face.

"What do you THINK you're DOINGGG? DO YOU have a PERmit?" They looked at each other, their arms sunk to the elbows in the mixture of earth and water.

"What do we need a permit for?" they said in unison. "You gonna git me in trouble," Afikomen said, wagging his finger at the sisters. "You know it!" In the distance the collard greens and radish plants spread luxuriously across the grass. "I'd like to be buried over there," Aaron told him, trying to get him off the subject of permits. "You must have a thing for swamp rats," he nodded toward his garden, laughing. "Over the fence then," she said. "Outside this place."

He laughed again. "You pining for Saint Elizabeth's?" he wanted to know. "Can't wait to git back?" Their two laughters twined about each other like the two wicks of the bridal candle, rose up into the trees, and settled alongside the prayers.

"You still need a permit," he said. "For what?" Aaron asked him. "For putting in that tree. Don't want no trees overshadowing the tombstones. Some Crankshaw relative fit to be tied. Can't show no partiality here," Afikomen went on.

"Oh that," Aaron said. "That's no tree, only a little bush. Won't amount to anything," she said, bending protectively over its four-foot rise, causing its branches, already budding, to fold over themselves, to shorten.

Whenever it got too crowded in the cemetery or the tree bent under the weight of the prayers, Afikomen would roll back a year. Slowly, slowly, one would fall away. Nineteen hundred years took a long time to get rid of. The hole in the cemetery filled up with them; they crowded upon one another until they spilled over the top of the hole and spread out along a hillside. Afikomen turned the crank until more of the years fell back. They swelled up in the conservative graveyard where the living wore prayer shawls and covered their heads and only prayed in Hebrew. The years fled through the wire gauge fence into the reform graveyard where everyone spoke in English and where the dead sat up from time to time to see what was happening. "We can't have this," the Orthodox rabbi shouted, seeing the years coming toward him from the two cemeteries.

"What about them?" Joseph demanded of Afikomen, pointing to the recently deceased, resting in their holes, the plastic green carpets covering the true grass and earth surrounding them. "What do they have to say about all of this?" she said, looking up the hill to the place where the long dead resided, where the infants had been buried, their tiny headstones long since hidden within the gutted trunks of old trees.

"Oh them, they don't bother me none," he told her. "On a day when I don't feel like working, they tell me not to bother. We gets on just fine.

On a day when I'm in the mood to work, they tell me 'That's good.' I keep track of the babies," he said, more to himself than to her.

On the road home Aaron and Joseph passed a dead squirrel. "That little squirrelly spirit is in God's hand now," Joseph said softly. "What did you say?" Aaron asked her.

"God isn't in heaven," Joseph ventured carefully. "I don't know where he is. And the squirrel isn't there on the road either; there's nothing left of him. By tomorrow we won't see any of him. But the squirrelly part, that's what God puts into his hand."

Closer to home, Aaron took her sister to see the leaves. Aaron parked the car and walked out to touch one. She held its huge green face in her arms, running her fingers along its smooth, rubbery surface. Up ahead, there was a year neither of them was likely to get to, a year when the centuries would fall back into the sleep of centuries, when the millennium would turn. Some would cross over that edge; some would never be able to look over it, the way Moses could not get a good view of Canaan, the way he could not walk into the place with his own feet. But that line was all they could think of now. It drew them toward itself, drew them forward like a huge magnet, iron filings like minutes, like years spilling toward the future.

LIKE A FIELD RIDDLED BY ANTS

Some people can do many things at a time without worrying, but as soon as I interrupt my work my heart feels sad, like a bookcase empty of books or a field riddled by ants.

—S. Y. Agnon

*A*t first, the interruptions were of no consequence. Like the locket of air contained in a keyhole. Later, they widened, like a doorway. Gradually the number of interruptions increased like the number of days that pass in a year until I felt in myself a constant yearning I could not name. As I moved through the long days, a certain tune accompanied me—the kind sung by the women suspended in the wire cages of the great mental institutions of long-gone days, desperate cries for help disguised in elaborate rhymes. The women—their pale faces pressed between the bars, their bony knuckles pushed up from beneath the skin like miniature heads of the cabalists pushing up from beneath their prayer shawls. Whatever I did the song commanded me. It grew ragged, insistent.

For what I did not claim of this world and shape in my hands—like the potter making from the dust his infinite shapes, like the Golem who rises from a few grains—I could not know. Like a swimmer who does not swim, my legs and arms forgot how to live in the water. They became suitable for the land alone. And I dreamed of water every night.

So I set about guarding my life. I built a fence around it. To the north I constructed a boundary of ice boulders. To the east, a wall of leaves. To the west, light. And to the south, water. Only the earth was allowed within. And what few birds could fly above the barriers I made for myself. And for many years I went on this way.

Gradually I began to listen to others. There came one day a man to my door who insisted on his claim for my attention. Perhaps, he urged, my message is of more consequence than the words you commit yourself to with such fervor. So from then on I listened anxiously for the stranger. Who, I wondered, could fall in to my realm from the world? Oh, how I longed for any disturbance: the slightest step in the hall, a rap on the window, a branch scratching aimlessly along the roof.

Why then should anticipation have caused me such grief? I dared not lift my pen to write a word, so poised was I for the possibility, for what might enter the silence. The ink dried in the inkwell. The tip of the pen hardened. The words fell back into that place where words begin to form. The dreams left my house and took up residence else-where.

Why do you regard what could happen with such morbid anxiety? Franz wants to know. When I, he goes on, hear the sounds of footsteps approaching my room, I listen eagerly to distinguish this pair of feet from all others. To flee from the miraculous, to avoid the unexpected—that is cowardice. In that one coming toward you is contained the perfect question, laying open every secret like a finger pointing the way. You may travel there when you discover whose footprints have walked through the sifted ash and who has rubbed against you wearing out your clothes and who surrounds you like a ridge around a field. What, you must say, of the world will this stranger offer me. What, that I wouldn't have access to myself.

Or my way, Johann urges me. Do you hear those donkeys braying in the middle of the tune I've just made up? They are the church fathers demanding that I make them a work of art. I have made them their music, a work we will never forget, though they do not know enough to realize how they have grown donkey's ears and tails. It is my own joke, he tells me.

Once, the guns started—rockets firing from the north. We who have fought over how the land should be used—whether for shelters or for growing carrots, potatoes, onions—fled not to the garden that had used up most of the space above ground, but to the shelter we had dug below ground. Down the concrete stairs we fled while the rockets sang overhead, down to the bunkers. I carried a child in one arm, a manuscript in the other. I was like the garden, only making a small concession to the rockets.

Even there, between the metal cots, in the dank stony air, I went on dreaming. The stories flew from my pen. No further interruptions; for were we not all gathered together, as under the tabernacle of fruits and vegetables in the ritual of the fall harvest. Only here we had no access to the star of morning, the first star of evening. We went on praying as though we could visualize the cosmos, though time was abolished in this place.

Now, I thought, nothing can disturb me. Not war, not the ominous footsteps. For there were no halls, no hidden spaces. Only a large room filled with bunks. But death visited us. And who cannot stop his scribbling for death.

The one death chose was not ready. And when death entered his body, he protested mildly at first and then with all his might until his wife and sons had to hold him down so he could succumb to the cold that climbed through the latticework of his body. Now who could say that this was not an interruption? Who could find fault with the stopping of work? That for a few days nothing more should be said. Or done.

And when they had committed him to the earth, time stopped again. The hands of the clock went around once, and once again. And then they rested. As on the sabbath, they did no more work. Only the laborers came to turn up the earth like sheets in a bed and make a place for him, among the others. Just as the men from the burial society had come the day before and taken his body and washed it and said their prayers over him.

When we came up from below ground and returned to our houses, we were grateful again for the air, for the song of the rockets whizzing by overhead to have ceased. In its place, the night songs of the cicadas. For it was their season. Everywhere one could see the swollen mounds where they had fled the earth for their brief sojourn above ground and the cycle by which they are born again. How they dared to shed their outermost garment, all that stood between them and the jaws of some rodent, we cannot say. But proof of it lay in the crisp exoskeletons attached to a leaf, while they themselves were elsewhere, above us. Drying, their white bodies hardening and taking on color until they became fully adult, they made ready to enter the choir above us, the buzz of throaty chanting back and forth among the poplars and eucalyptus trees.

In the early morning, I came upon a brother of the cicada, a bright green beetle with patches of iridescence and shading along its back in precisely the arrangement of color in the yew bushes. The beetle lay helplessly on its back wheeling its legs in the air. I brought a twig near for it to grasp and twirled it around so the creature was upright once more and set it upon the yew bush, noticing as I did how its antennae ended in a three-pronged structure that could expand and contract at will. I thought no more about the green beetle, other than to acknowledge the small voice within that uttered a final "God's handiwork" as I parted from it and went back to work.

But later that night, long after midnight, I was returning to my house, nothing for company but a piece of a moon and a few clouds and that endless choir of cicadas, when I put the key into the lock and heard a sudden cry of distress. I looked down to see that in my approach I had injured a cicada. It lay on its back, its enormous wings under it like the palette used to carry the wounded. Its bright green body, the black shading, and under all of it a thin trail of mucus.

Oh those wings, lacework of veins like the threads of a girl's long hair when it flows in a river and, connecting it all, that substance like translucent glass stretched across its frame.

The creature cried out when it was struck. Cried out only once and lay still. Who has said that insects feel no pain? Here was proof then. And that small cry seared into me. I opened the door and went in. And did nothing more about it.

What does the Talmud say? Do not leave your brother on the steps to suffer his pain alone. But bring him into your house that he may take nourishment with you and refresh himself.

In my sleep that night I, who had long ago given up dreaming of cigarettes, was smoking a cigarette while around me families of cicadas were emerging from the dust and rising into the rafters, singing.

So there are those things which rise up from the earth and approach us. And that which falls to us from above. There are the celestial cities which hover over our own cities; there are the underpinnings of the world which hold us aloft. We had once held that what came to us from below, from out of the earth, was good, the harvest in its season. And what fell upon us from above was good as well. For who has not longed to catch a glimpse of Ezekiel's wheel humming with angels and figures from the other world? Or to see the Messiah being brought forth out of the land, made of the fervent prayers of generations though Elijah's offices.

But what came this day, what rose up from the earth and entered the heavens and came down to us was not that which we longed for, which we waited for during the times of our greatest suffering. For it was man-made. The first who beheld it were the herds of reindeer in the north. The particles fell upon them as they moved into their summer hunting grounds. But so imperceptibly they were unaware of it. And into the milk of the females. And into the cells of them all, so that the peoples of the north could no longer feed their young from the reindeer as they had for over three thousand years.

And in the warmer climates, high up in the mountains, the summer crops were being prepared and harvested and stored for the winter. The milk from the goats was drying in the sun; the cheese was ripening on the porches. The potatoes were being pulled from the earth. And the legumes were drying. The particles fell upon these things. And the small mouths on the undersides of leaves that drew to themselves moisture and certain gasses welcomed the new element whose particles crept into them. And in the light that flowed from the west the particles came, coloring the sky. Never was the sunset more beautiful than now. And in the blue glaciers, the particles drifted and entered as though all the doors of the houses had been left open.

And those who dwelled in this world went streaming out of their habitats: from their caves and their ice houses, from the trees and valleys, all who could crawl out of the sea, and those in the mountains, all went out over the earth in search of some place of safety.

For my part I have gone back into the house, my body bearing its own share of the particles, enough for myself and my descendants. Even now the changes are being wrought in places too small to visualize. Even now the interruption continues and I yield to it as though it had something to offer me, some wisdom or message if only I could read it.

And we all of us coat the earth with our shapes like a field that bears the motion of ants—quick signals where only moments before they had been—the quivering instantaneous signals of their passage as they swarm over the field on their way to reconstruct what has been broken into, as they hurry on their way to fill out whatever form and shape the future has devised.

My Companion the Aleph-Bet

I once made a pact with myself: I would buy the first volume of the Babylonian Talmud, make poems of it, and read it, not so much as a scholar or religionist, but in the manner of the poet, grazing here and there, attracted by one passage, skipping the next, remembering days later a phrase or a word, trying always to imagine the sound of the voice that spoke a particular portion.

Of course it was second best. My dream had been to read the Talmud in its original languages: first the Torah portion, fixed to the center of the page, itself the core, the heart. Around it, the dialogues, the discussions, the blessed and crooked conversations. Rashi to the left, the Tosafists to the right, the more contemporary additions set out of the way in the back. Somewhere in my memory was the ancient Geniza of Cairo where the souls of the books were kept in a chamber in the earth. Those discarded books, too worn for use, too holy to destroy.

I settle for English, always feeling cheated by my lack of drive and by my accident of birth in the Diaspora. Had I been born elsewhere, I might very well not have been alive now. Therefore I will only complain briefly about being outside the heart's place for a Jew, cut off from the language and religion that might have taken up the slack in his eternal longing, a longing he cannot name or define. It is akin to the longing Plato speaks of in the Symposium, a longing that is not lost by the coming together of two souls. Longing is a condition of being alive. But to know that doesn't help. Indeed, it takes more and more elaborate forms as one grows older.

I would like to buy the first volume of the Babylonian Talmud, I told the bookstore owner. He looked at me, disbelieving, just as he had looked at me the year before when I told him that I wanted to buy a shofar. He had asked which organization I represented. I said that it was for my husband's birthday, that he had always wanted a shofar. Once past his initial shock, the owner agreed that it was an unusual idea, that perhaps this would be the beginning of a good thing. But the Talmud is different. He seemed suspicious and concerned, as though I were breaking an ancient taboo. What, after all, did a woman want with such a book? In the synagogue the women traditionally read the Tzena u-Re'ena, the book written in Yiddish that deals with matters pertaining to women, read as they sat upstairs in the synagogue separated from the men. Hadn't I my grandmother's own copy, the small black book with an embossed cover and yellowed pages that I so cherished? My eldest sister had given it to me at the time of my mother's death.

I could imagine his thoughts. Here was this woman asking him to break the set of the Soncino edition of the Babylonian Talmud, to sell her the first volume, Zera'im (Seeds). The book deals in the first part with the prescribed forms for saying the blessings, and in the second with the laws regarding the planting, harvesting, and division of the fields. Even such practical matters as where a pious man shall put his tefillin when he goes to use the public privy are considered. In Berakoth we read:

> Beth Hillel says, He keeps them in his hand and enters. R. Akiba said: He holds them in his garment and enters. In his garment, do you say? Sometimes they may slip out and fall! Say rather, he holds them in his hand and in his garment, and enters, and he puts them in a hole on the side of the privy, but he should not put them in a hole on the side of the public way, lest they should be taken by passersby, and he should render himself suspect. For a certain student once left his tefillin in a hole adjoining the pubic way, and a harlot passed by and took them, and she came to the Beth ha-Midrash and said: See what So-and-so gave me for my hire, and when the student heard it, he went to the top of a roof and threw himself down and killed himself. Thereupon they ordained that a man should hold them in his garment and in his hand and then go in.

The bookstore owner finally agreed to sell me the book; a strange thing happened afterward. Months later he went to order another whole set of the Babylonian Talmud and it arrived missing the first volume. In his eyes from that day onward I was a danger.

April is not only the cruelest month, but the most impossible. Into the midst of cold comes a month wrapped in light; the air itself seems visible to the naked eye. The heart steeled against winter becomes vulnerable again. The attitudes of others, the ordinary hug or brush with a friend are magnified. The soul goes bravely into a world it dares not trust. It cannot help itself. Everything invites it.

For a Jew, a great sorrow hovers in the world in April: April 1943, the uprising in the Warsaw ghetto. Of the three million Jews of Poland, of the community that had existed there for one thousand years, the end came through systematic deportations to concentration camps and death by gassing, shooting, torture, and starvation by the Germans. Ridding the Warsaw ghetto of its Jews was to be a gift to Adolf Hitler for his birthday. The body of an entire people turned to ash in the crematoria of Poland and Germany. If the Holocaust was the answer, what could the question have been? For what have the lives been taken? What the cause to explain the murders of a million children?

In April, Passover. The exodus from Egypt, the passage of our people out of slavery. My children are not at home for the first time since they were born. My father is not with us. My mother, only in spirit. There are changes in our Seder. We are older. The aunt who had been well the year before has had a stroke. She rests her head on the table as our leader begins to recount the story of Joseph, his namesake. Joseph, the son of Jacob, Joe begins. The aunt says to no one in particular: Yes, I knew him well. Joe Jacobs, my student. Joe Jacobs, the boxer, the prize-fighter who never won a fight. And Joseph went down to the land of Egypt, Joe continues, cast out by his brothers. Yes, the aunt went on, he was despised by his family. And Joseph had a dream, our leader continued. Joe Jacobs was a dreamer, the aunt said, sitting bolt upright. Her counterpoint to the service reminded me of the interference that had always seemed an essential part of the Seder. Either it was the children telling us to hurry, that they were hungry, or an adult saying: When do we get to the soup, the egg? The service needed to be long enough for us to feel that we had gone through an experience together, that we had truly endured something, a token of what our forefathers had endured. And that the children had taken part, had sung the Four Questions, and had been welcomed into this commemorative, at the same time living, ritual.

Surely to the Talmudist, the act of writing or studying the commentaries was not an occasional highlight in his life, but a necessity. I know, I am always told, that the shtetl was no picnic, that life was cruel. I know from a few isolated facts told to me by my mother and father that life in this country for their parents was harsh and often without hope. So if I am infatuated with a true Shabbat meal that contains the blessings over the bread and wine, the lighting of the candles, and concludes with the singing of Hebrew melodies, I ask to be forgiven.

And if I prefer not to see the kinds of sacrifices that the woman must make for all of this to happen each week, I hope my companion feminists will forgive me.

And if for me the joy of the evening comes at the end of the meal—when the host reads to me in Yiddish and then paraphrases in English the poem whose narrator bends down to lift ash and dust from under his shoe to see if we are truly descended from that dust, that ash, which he lifts to his nose to smell, to his mouth to taste, preferring the notion of the living spirit, *ruach,* which brings life to us and leaves us when we die, so be it.

For me, that spirit appeared one day on a commuter train between Dunellen and Elizabeth, New Jersey, early one morning in the form of a boy hovering just at puberty. I sit next to him because he is wearing a yarmulke.

I hesitate for a long time to speak with him. For fear of what? As though I were still standing in Jerusalem in Mea Shearim in the bakery shop one October, Sukkot, buying a honey cake to bring to friends. To my right, the men draw back from me, and the women and young girls lean to the left. They are each like the halves of the Red Sea, parted, and I walk through untouched. Physical contact might be a sin. Perhaps I am menstrually unclean.

I think of this as I sit next to the boy on the train. And I feel another reservation, that of the parent who had always cautioned her own children against speaking to strangers. But the time on the train is running out and there are some things I want to know. What school do you go to? I hear myself ask the boy. He names the school by its initials. I do not recognize them. I catch a glimpse of something working in him, something serious and complicated as I look into green eyes. The face is already animated by thought.

I suddenly think of the broken lives I have witnessed, lives that move by vague indirection ungoverned by personal codes or by goals. And I think of my young neighbor on the train. I try to imagine his three older brothers who have each gone to Israel before him. When it was finally his turn, his family had become expert at the journey. He tells me about his bar mitzvah at the Western Wall, about Rashi and the Chumesh, his pronunciation comfortable and familiar. And he tells me how he does not greatly like his school and will commute to New York next year as his brothers had. I ask if all his courses are in Hebrew, and he carefully explains that the concepts in the commentaries are very difficult and that the teacher has the students learn various Hebrew phrases, which he intersperses with English. Are there many students at your school? I ask him. (I had been doing some rapid calculations. Now if there is this child and his three brothers and the two boys in the seat in front who attend this school, perhaps the future will be better than I'd thought. If you add to these few a whole school of such youngsters, perhaps the world will manage well enough.) Oh yes, he answers, there are many students, perhaps twenty in each class, in the upper grades even more. I do not show my disappointment.

I am less interested in trying to decipher the social revolution we are going through. I know that I am very interested in how a small boy with green eyes shapes his life and how that life is governed by principles that include learning and thought and goals that he will look forward to meeting. I think of the way the smallest possibility in this boy is drawn forth and developed. I think suddenly of the beautiful intricate shapes of the bony cells of the femur, the bone that joins the lower leg to the hip. The longest and strongest bone of the body is composed of a series of interlocking arches like those of a Gothic cathedral, capable of supporting the entire weight of the upright body, just as the Talmud has supported our people through the centuries.

It is said that the afterlife is composed of a great library, the books arranged in the order of their holiness, and when a new book is found worthy, the other books on the shelf squeeze together to provide room. So in this life we welcome the child on the train bearing the words of the fathers in the early morning. In him we have the measured contentions of the commentators who spoke about a world worthy of their faith— a world mysterious enough to earn their inextinguishable curiosity.

Note: As in Jewish tales, one day I had a phone call from a couple who believed the boy I had written about was their son. Perhaps it was so.

The World Is a Parchment Scrawled with Words

KHAMSIN

*T*his is the age of exile. Within the boundaries of homeland we dream of escape. And when we have gone out of the land, we cannot breathe in the new atmosphere; we long for homeland.

For some, exile is imposed from without: war, famine, an untenable political regime, overwhelming pressure from the state whose requirements come before the individual's, including the sacrifice of sons and daughters.

And when the exile is not geographical, as with the Marranos, the one in exile appears to observe the outward norms all the while clinging to a people or a language, to the values and shared memories of a lost world that holds sway over him.

Or as Moshe Dor writes in *Khamsin*[1] (literally *fifty,* a hot desert wind originating in the Sahara, so intense as to alter perception of color and light), "Poets go into exile from interior exile . . . the land of exile is the motherland." Or in his poem "Town":

The town of my birth is the town where
I live, my guarantee against the anxieties
of immigrants . . .

Why then, when the mulberries
unscroll their sticky bright sprouts
am I filled with nostalgia for towns
where I wasn't born, won't ever live?

This exile lends to the poet's voice the anguish of dislocation, resignation, longing, and irony. He looks in from the outside, though he exists in the center of the fire. Like the dreamer who is both observing and observed, the poet is the central actor and audience at the same instant. He negotiates the distance between the two like one who swims for his life in a turbulent sea.

And how is it to live in this condition? In "Shelter" Moshe Dor writes:

We cleaned out the bomb shelter,
a municipal edict too stringent
to ignore. We worked diligently:

. . .

Now we can wait
for evil from any direction. Only
our image reflected in that sliver
of mirror is slightly blurred, perhaps
because we have let down our guard.

A prophetic poem—witness the SCUD missiles not long ago volleying forth to Israel from Iraq's western fringe—filled with the longing for normalcy, with what it means to live on the edge.

Vigilance: Perhaps that is the lodestone of these poems. Behind Israel's struggle for and achievement of the kind of life we, in more neutral territory, take for granted is that eye always open. To live that way for one's whole life exacts an extraordinary price. It is said that God is like the fish of the sea, with eyes always open. But it is not God's domain that requires vigilance. It is man's: this homeland that Moshe Dor is made from, this wilderness. This oasis that is the land of Israel, this sea made in the shape of a harp. These mountains. These stones into which the sun pours its life. And out of which light goes back into the atmosphere. He is made of this land and it infuses every poem he writes.

In "Identifying Marks," the poem asks why Byzantium has fallen when it could have survived a siege with its "granaries . . . overflowing,/ the walls" that "might have borne the impact/ of Turkish cannonballs." And there is even the rumor of rescue by the Italians. Ah, how well we know about one country looking after another! "How to explain Metropolis' fall," he writes. "Historians say one small gate was left unlatched, perhaps/ from simple oversight. Through that gate/ the Sultan's force penetrated the city."

In every image does the force of history ignite. Though it is Byzantium we remember Herod's fortress and the mass suicide of the Hebrews, we remember the fall of Jerusalem and the exile to Babylon, the lament of Jeremiah. On neutral territory, centuries later, the poet examines the shards of defeat: Constantine's "purple sandals" by which his corpse is identified.

"One small gate . . . left unlatched": Doors, gates, these are Israel's trademarks—Mea Shearim, the place of 100 gates; the Golden gate sealed until resurrection; Jaffa gate, the Dung gate; the gates of the cabala. Ancient and modern, entwined. And the poignancy, the impossibility of salvation from enemies through the use of gates, the irony of airborne missiles, air that heretofore carried the likes of Ezekiel or the signs of covenant.

Here are poems that explore the terror of the creative act for "what would ripen, like/ a terrible fetus," poems in which skinheads inhabit the same space as Orpheus but cannot hear him. And here is the language: "I . . . fortify myself behind 22 protective fences,/ *aleph, bet, gimmel.*" And our companions, found and lost: "No, it will not be I traversing the brambles of your sleep/ to lead the caravan./ Earth is stronger."

Here, not only the son in exile but the motherland too is submerged: "I think tomorrow,/ surely by the day after,/ the signal to return will come/ from the drowned motherland." In an essay written during the celebration of Tel Aviv's birthday, the son cannot find his city for the changes: "The little houses have disappeared. The bells on the camels' long necks are silent. The horizon is hidden behind tall buildings. My Tel Aviv is hiding . . . She hides, and I seek her, in love and despair."

Here, the struggle for speech so that it may be offered in love, "I breathe effortlessly/ and lead an infinite column/ of words, all clearly enunciated/ . . . to create/ the alphabet anew so that I/ may utter now to you, beloved."

And here, in essays, we find a kind of Kunstlerroman, the writer protagonist in a life-and-death struggle toward maturity and his artistic mission, a form most unusual among Israeli writers and particularly important in the way it documents the parallel struggle of Israel's rebirth and maturation.

Vigilance. The land. Language and history. The power of love. Exile. A boy who tears at the wild vines which entrap him, like the ram of Abraham caught in the thicket. Escape and return. The soul of a man struggling between the outlines of his life and the life of his nation whose days and nights mingle in a vortex of Biblical proportions: Moshe Dor, *Khamsin*.

NIGHT WATCH

1

We use language, according to Hayim Nahman Bialik, to conceal. We are like one "who crosses a river when it is breaking up, by stepping across floating, moving blocks of ice. Between the breaches the void looms."[2]

"The Holocaust," poet Barbara Goldberg writes, "was the uninvited guest. Greedy and sly, it gobbled up everything." She is the daughter of survivors, the granddaughter of those who could not imagine another life long enough to escape in time. Though more than thirty years old when she realized she was a poet, she "had excellent training in reading between the lines. I was aware of how language can obscure as well as reveal. Obsessed from childhood with curiosity about the 'underbelly' of things, I wanted to find a way to penetrate surface appearances." Her legacy? "To stay liquid, be able to make a quick getaway. . . . Fear is the ravenous wolf at my door. Sometimes I throw him a scrap, in the shape of a poem."

2

"On the other side of the barrier of language, behind its curtain, stripped of its husk of speech," writes Bialik, "the spirit of man wanders ceaselessly . . . the word's existence takes place by virtue of the process by which it closes up the small aperture of the void, constructing a barrier to prevent the void's darkness from welling up and overflowing its bounds."

Yet the poet must use the same language of concealment to pry open the aperture in order that the face of the void may be seen. For what is poetry if not words that have looked into the night? Words that return to us in the morning, bearing the signs of the struggle, like that of Jacob and his angel. And if that darkness is the face of the mystery that bounds our life—our existence prior to life, our inevitable extinguishing—if that is the eternal condition of being alive, surely it is worthy of the poet's words.

3

Of what is this barrier against the void constructed? "Give desire a shape," the poet tells us. "Fierce longings" keep us temporarily out of the eye of darkness. Even our "terrible hunger/ which would fill . . . the pockets of Grandfather's voluminous coat" is only prelude to the real danger, a rehearsal perhaps to forestall the final absence.

And entertain that desire, "no matter/ if that shape be squalor or sailor . . ." The imperative voice of the title poem, "Night Watch" is quite literally constructing a premise and a world before our eyes: "Give him moves . . . foreknowledge. . . . Make it night." Here is the stage, the theater, the setting; here are the players. And here is our narrator to guide us: "You choose this drama to unfold/ as monologue, the way you will/ replay this scene, your fierce/ longing, and how you were taken." Prologue, anticipation, consummation—the essential ingredients of any good story. All bundled into twenty brief lines, and all inviting the reader to commence this journey.

4

Hunger makes its presence felt in many incarnations. Whether as a "hunger for clarity,/ a fish swimming out of its bones" or in the fear of that "terrible hunger" being exposed, or in its various disguises: "Love,/ sometimes when you enter/ I bare my teeth. Salt/ / or sweet? The body decides/ since the body must answer/ to curious, various hungers." Or in her narrator's identification with a doe who

> with a bound . . . clears the wire
> barrier between woodland and garden,
> devouring begonias in search of sumac
> and sassafras. So merciless
> in her hunger, I suddenly think, Sister,
> are we so very different, craving,
> as we do, surfeit for the belly,
> buckskin for the back.
>
> from "The Succulent Edge"[3]

In "First There was Light and That Begins the Narrative" no sooner is hunger invented than it must deal with its consequences: "Then there was hunger, then/ there was blame. Even God must/ be ambivalent about knowing." "First," the poet tells us, "there was light and that began/ the narrative. All events,/ a fulfillment. Even mistakes."

5

In "Marvelous Pursuits," a playful sonata elaborate as music, its sound repetitions echoing in the hall of memory ("Her angelic son, runt of the litter,/ plays Scarlatti after sunset, balding/ pate glowing like an unhatched egg."), its tale of mistresses and infidelities leads us back to the generative moment: "Anima, animus, we/ descend into our evolutionary niche,/ wild, demonic, from the bliss of it." The tone is ironic, a full drama unfolds. A counterweight to annihilation, the potent country: our vital center, our sexuality.

"I like to think," writes Goldberg, "that all the machinations, time-consuming rituals, delaying tactics, are propitiations to the god Eros, whom we must appease before we can gain admittance to the darkroom. Eros resides in the darkroom . . ." But then, once we have entered the room of Eros, we find Psyche where "wounding, reflection, and insight are inevitable. For she eventually comes with her lamp." The process of entering and making the poem is united with the poem's use against annihilation, the "scrap" flung against the void, appeasing it at the same time as it gains entry.

6

If desire and our various hungers (the signs of our own vitality) help to constitute the barriers we construct against the void, it is in the transformation of these vital signs that we attempt to penetrate the unknowable. In "Excursion," Barbara Goldberg writes: "How easily we seem to abandon./ our port of origin, bearing ourselves/ to a foreign sun. . . . we want to own/ the way of seeing that underlies/ a language, as if we could put on/ a new life by slipping into another/ mother tongue." Desire, says the poet, is "nothing but the will to own, not/ the body, but the mind/ it inhabits," but then she turns it another way: No, "not/ the mind but how it talks/ its cadences, the way/ of seeing that underlies/ a language." And another stage of transformation: "as if we could put on/ another life by learning how/ it garners information."

And if the dance of human relationship is not sufficient, then the poet offers us the dance of the mind. In "A Former Philosophy Student Addresses Issues Raised by Her Professor," our narrator asks, "How do we know what we know?" She admonishes us to "surpass the seductiveness of the visible . . . the glistening/ moisture on a purple grape." Forsake the visible for "the next/ order of being, that ideal state where/ things dwell in their thingness," but soon enough we are thrust into the "dark epicenter/ of chaotic disarray." And as she has chosen for her poetry abundant profusion, so in the section "Metaphysics" she asks if ultimate reality is "singular./ stark, austere, or polygamous,/ flamboyant as a hot flamenco," and her answer: "Consider it all." In the section "Aesthetics," apart from the subtle machinations, the search for the "shade of meaning," the poet cannot help reaching "for/ the milky white pearl inside, then/ wringing the sense out."

Poet Stanley Kunitz once described the empty page as "the cold bed of the page" when thinking of the aural aspect of the poet's language and the difficulty of sustaining the poetry's sound when committed to paper. Barbara Goldberg's wonderfully vital poetry is meant for the ear. Watch how sound lifts these poems back to our hearing. And note how the elaborate desire-dance of these poems, barrier to the void and point of entry, is what we call our *life*.

A JOURNAL FOR JOHN HOLMES

*John Holmes, beloved teacher-poet at Tufts University,
always had his poetry writing students keep journals. In
the spirit of that tradition, and as a way to honor this
generous teacher, to acknowledge writing as a process
always in the state of becoming, I continue his teaching
this way, as a journal.*

AUGUST 12, 1996: The word was that if your poem was good it
was a one-grunt poem. And if it was very good, it was a two-
grunt poem. And if superb, it rated three grunts from John
Holmes. The truth was, as articulate as he was through his
writing, as alive in his words, so he was reticent in person. In
those days, I was almost pathologically shy. The biweekly meet-
ings under the eaves in Packard Hall to review the two-weeks'
worth of journals and not quite born poems were often studies
in silence. Yet they meant more to me than all the anatomy labs
I was taking: more than histology, which I loved: infinitely more
than organic chemistry, which I was taking with Paul Doleman
who had taught my father before me (my father being far more
successful than I, good enough in fact to go into biochemistry

for a lifetime). I was not alone in this. I knew of others who grew and strengthened under John Holmes's inarticulate tutelage. John Ciardi was one such person—student of Holmes, translator of Dante, poet and essayist, for years columnist for the *Saturday Review*, "Manner of Speaking."

Once, Holmes told me, he had gone to visit John Ciardi's mother. John Ciardi stepped out of the room for a moment and Mrs. Ciardi— who had been a fierce mother, slinging burning cooking pots across the room in anger, John having been an early breadwinner, stealing apples and other sundries for the family's repasts—used the opportunity to inquire of John Holmes a question that had surely been on her mind for years. "My son," she asked, "is he good?"

John Holmes wasn't sure what she meant. Was she asking if her son had become a good man, a true man? Or was it that she wondered if he was held in high repute because of his poetry, his writing? Was that it? John Holmes never did quite figure out what was behind the carefully sent question. But after a long moment, the kind of silence he was capable of, the silence that one could settle down to and take comfort from, John Holmes looked at Ciardi's mother, looked carefully into her eyes and said reassuringly: "Your son, your son John Ciardi is good." That was all she needed.

SEPTEMBER 4, 1996: Anne Sexton, Maxine Kumin, George Starbuck and John Holmes met in a workshop in the late 1950s. Anne Sexton had taken a class with John Holmes in 1958. In describing a poem she had written for Holmes, Anne Sexton talks about what she has left out: "I didn't say that you have taught me everything I do know about poetry, and taught me with a firm patience and a kind smile. And I didn't say that poetry has saved my life; has given me a life and if I had not wandered in off the street and found you and your class, that I would indeed be lost." This acknowledgment comes in the face of Anne Sexton's awareness of John Holmes's disapproval of her public exposure of herself and family. Later, she implores him: "Please, John, stop making me feel like a toad ... Oh my, this toad suit is very uncomfortable."[4]

SEPTEMBER 9, 1996: In a wonderful anthology of love poems, *A Little Treasury of Love Poems: From Chaucer to Dylan Thomas*, which John Holmes edited and introduced, Holmes begins: "The shortest and most important love-letter ever written said: 'Tonight, same place, same time.' Was the language of that miniature classic Latin, or Babylonian, or was it pencilled and pushed into a Brooklyn mailbox? A girl in Nebraska knew where to find it, and a lady in Elizabeth's court; both, in some secret place." A poem Holmes had written, "Take Home This Heart," included in this collection begins this way: "Take home this travelled heart. It has been lost./ It has been wandering in the world alone . . ." The final stanza goes this way: "Take home my heart, and take it into yours,/ And light the waiting fire, and close the doors,/ And let me in the firelight touch your face,/ And tell you love has led me to this place."[5]

SEPTEMBER 10, 1996: In *Writing Poetry* John Holmes cautions: "But never trust a poet. He is silent like a bomb. He is motionless like a gyroscope. When nothing much seems to be going on, a tremendous great deal is going to happen. Of course, he may merely be thinking about his clothes, or his car. He does have his human moments. . . . But his habit saves him, his involuntary reaction; like the barest blob of an amoeba, he opens himself, closes on the metaphor and years later he writes it."[6]

SEPTEMBER 12, 1996: The last time I saw John Holmes, the last memory I have of this man who so strongly helped to shape and confirm my identity as a writer is of his presence beside me. We were in the audience of what was called "A Celebration of Poets," the second of two Poetry Festivals—which included R. P. Blackmur, Yvor Winters, Marianne Moore, Mark Van Doren, John Holmes, May Sarton, Richard Eberhart, Richard Wilbur, and Randall Jarrell—at The Johns Hopkins University. John Holmes had delivered his poet's lecture, "Surroundings and Illuminations," and had come to sit near me. I remember to this day the strength of his presence, the comfort of his silence, the sense one had of the vitality of his language taking shape beneath the silence. "The poet is not poet of himself alone, except in that last hour when he writes his poem. The poet writing, and the poet living his ordinary days, is ringed about by powers and influences. Whether he is affected by them, or with full awareness rejects them, the poet is a center of surroundings and illuminations."[7] Unlike Frost's couplet: "We dance around in a ring and suppose, But the Secret sits in the middle and knows," Holmes uses the metaphor of Stonehenge to teach us that the poet sets his surround: "recovered pillars," "the never-forgotten direction toward the sun," "barrows, layered with those objects that outlast man: tools; small hard works of art; and bones of the body," "evidence of incredible effort, generations of inexhaustible labor, and triumphs of constructive cunning."

Holmes put the poet at the center; the "surroundings" are made of "active intelligence recording, evaluating, and discoursing upon poetry," the "illuminations" are made by those "perpetuators who love, and teach, and explain poetry."

OCTOBER 1, 1996: Once I found an opportunity to thank John Holmes. I was in graduate school at Johns Hopkins. I gathered together all of the letters John had sent me over the years and all the poetry of his I could find and presented his work to my fellow students in the Writing Seminars there, taught by another wonderful teacher, Elliott Coleman, who had founded the Seminars a quarter century earlier. Strange to think that neither that essay nor the letters can be found in time for this writing about John Holmes. How does one thank a teacher who has made the difference? And who has done so at a time when it had the most impact on the student's life. He had a way of letting us know that we should take this way of looking at the world seriously. That it was worthy of our abiding attention. Not just now, not just then, but for the rest of our time on this earth. Through all the harrowing that being alive involves. And through all that is affirming.

But what is it that a writer leaves behind for us? We need not invent his life. For he has left a trace, a hieroglyph, rich and telling. He has left us his writing. So this son of a civil engineer, so fond of making, constructing his poetry and so fascinated by how things are made in this world—his students will remember the wonderful trips to the stained-glass makers—handled words like wood and nails, like tools well kept and cared for, ready when needed. And these tools carried the dark tide of his life straining its banks to overwhelm him, kept in abeyance by his life in art, by the shaping of his poems, by the constancy of his communication through letters to many of us, by his teaching.

And when he tried to burrow down beneath good tidings to that dark river that he knew, when in "The Fortune Teller,"[8] the narrator is told that he will "move in love/ Among many who love you," that his fears will be gone, that he will write and that his children will be safe, his voice calls "Stop! Stop!" He asks for the "terrible truth of my palm,/ The furrows of grief, the clatter of calamity,/ time's roof crashing, my very home my doom,/ My poison myself." This latter-day Job girds himself for the truth while the fortune-teller claims that "Nothing will be taken. You walk in light./ Your cry is heard." The narrator acknowledges: "But I was saying it, it was in my mouth a noise/ As if I had been dead, and now was not dead."

And so the resurrection into life. He gives this title poem its central place in this collection. But there are others. From "Order Clearly Asking," the poet's way of sensing the journey, of following it out to find what is there: "I have never forgotten a man who, planning a road, / First built the hill in modeling clay on a board,/ And ran his right thumb-end down around the slope,/ The easy, the easiest way, as if to feel how the hill/ Wanted it . . . The man did nothing but find it."

OCTOBER 16, 1996: In a letter written to me on this very day in 1954, John Holmes said: "I think all my hurts have been by death—that of my first wife, of men I greatly cared for like Charles Gott, and John Cousens, and Albert Kahn, of my father and my mother—or by a painful separation—a broken engagement, girls I loved who stopped loving me, friends who moved far away, and fell into silence. . . . I live in a sort of constant vigilance lest anything happen to my wife or any of my children—and, for their sakes, lest anything happen to me. I literally don't care what happens to me, but I don't want Johnny to lose his father, having lost his mother. What I was saying about Robinson's poems, about the secret word written on the heart, the hidden wound, I was saying about myself. The hidden wound is a strength, an armor against all further hurt." Holmes goes on to talk about the way poetry was his release, that it saved him. He was able to talk with his deceased wife directly and to look ahead to his life. "I freed myself, by this poem ("Next Year's Music"), from what I had been doing for six months, re-living the night of her death, rehearsing it. It broke the dark spell, and let me go forward." Holmes talks then about being able to begin his relationship with Doris Kirk, whom he married in June of 1948 to his great happiness.

The 1954 letter concludes with his rendition of a charming conversation with his wonderful three-month-old daughter Margaret in which he claims to have aired his "views about Toynbee's philosophy of history compared with Whitehead's views on man's place in the universe. Margaret was right with me every step of the way. That is, she understood as much of what I was talking about as I did, and again, and very wisely, said, Aaaalg. Uh. Mmmm. Llllll." And then the letter ends with a characteristic recognition of the other, a remembering that he is writing to a quite young woman and in a diffident humorous way, as though to bring the conversation back to a place where, with grace, he can close the letter: "If there is anything I would like to do that I can't do or be, it is to play the piano as well as you do."

OCTOBER 17, 1996: If it is true—if what John Ciardi has written about
Holmes's sense of his place in the world of writers is so, of not achiev-
ing the recognition he might have wished for—let it be so that at last
we permit the poems to speak for the man, to become visible as his fit-
ting memory, these "word things," as Bill Stafford has called them.
From "A Wish"[9]:

> To be remembered in wood
> Knifed out following a grain
> Shaped the way its tree stood.
> Not painted. Not rubbed. Plain.
> From the small rings and low bole.
> And I think not my carven face
> But some clench of a root, burl
> Slow grown without much grace.
> It might mean by lift and mass
> How I was heavy, how I was hard,
> Though sun up grain could pass
> To streak a memorial marred
> Block of a cut and common wood.
> Let some blade bite, in a hand
> Trying timber, if it could—
> Ring, color, knot, strand—
> Seem me and be wild wood.

In the patient making, out of the plain elements of a human life, out of
daily attentiveness, out of silence, did this good man and his work take
form. What luck to have been—even for a little—part of his generous
company! And to have, for whatever years are left, his poetry.

There is so much left out here—how he brought his students into
contact with the best of American poetry and poets. I treasured the read-
ings—which were unusual in those days—and the gatherings afterward
at his home. He took us and our work seriously. He was an excellent
model for us through his own constant association with his muse,
through his daily writing and active life as writer-teacher, through his
expectations of us. I think of him often after all these years. I carry him
with me in my life.

In "The Fear of Dying," the narrator has no intention of being present for the dying: "I'll send myself a green wreath, I'll send a wreath/ All green, deserved, but not be there for that death." When we lost him, when he went on ahead of us at fifty-eight, it seemed he was not wholly gone from us. From whatever place the dead inhabit, his words stream back to us.

From Alexandria to
American Via Amtrak

I was once on a train heading north along the Hudson River
when the conductor sent out a clarion call over the loudspeaker:
"Who knows the Seven Wonders of the Ancient World? A prize
for the winner!" For a split second I couldn't imagine where I
was. It was the kind of question I had dreamed of being asked.
But here? On a train on the East Coast of America? People
started making their offerings. The lottery? The Parthenon?
Pimlico Racetrack? Armageddon? Mount Rushmore? The
repeal of Prohibition? A small group gathered in the Café Car.
We pooled what we knew: The Great Pyramid of Giza? The
Hanging Gardens of Babylon? By the time we'd reached our des-
tination, we had a few of the Wonders. The conductor decided
to reward the entire small band in the Café Car: Cokes all the
way around.

A talk given at the rededication of the American University Library,
April 21, 1999.

Thus the Great Library of Alexandria entered my consciousness. Scrolls of parchment and papyrus tucked into pigeonholes. Callimachus' divisions into ten halls, each devoted to a branch of literature, science, or philosophy, and later, Greek and Roman sections. And later still, *armaria,* those wooden chests for storing manuscripts, clothed in linen or leather jackets. The apocryphal burning of the library during Julius Caesar's occupation with the loss of the most complete collection of Greek and Near Eastern literature, a matter still debated today. This cosmopolitan city that drew people from many regions; the library a meeting place for the exchange of culture and learning.

Perhaps Borges had Alexandria in mind when he wrote his story, "The Library of Babel."[10] "The universe," he writes "(which others call the Library) is composed of an indefinite and perhaps infinite number of hexagonal galleries . . ." The letters on the spines of the books do not "indicate or prefigure what the pages will say." In this scenario, man is the imperfect librarian, the library or universe the work of a god. The books appear to be impenetrable. At first, when it was "proclaimed that the Library contained all books, the first impression was one of extravagant happiness. All men felt themselves to be the masters of an intact and secret treasure. There was no personal or world problem whose eloquent solution did not exist in some hexagon" of the library. The story concludes with a footnote in which the narrator attributes to a Letizia Alvarez de Toledo the summation that this "vast library is useless . . . a single volume would be sufficient . . . containing an infinite number of infinitely thin leaves." But perhaps Borges' conclusion prefigures the place we've come to, the infinitely miniaturizing computer chip, the single volume that can contain what we claim as our world culture's knowledge.

Some say it was not the Alexandrine library but a lighthouse that qualified as one of the Wonders. But I choose to claim a library as a wonder of the ancient world. And of the modern world as well. What began as a library for a few—like the ancient temples of religion—has become a democratic place of learning for all citizens. A free and public offering that all could partake of—though as Richard Wright once wrote, learning was not a privilege granted to all of our citizens, and his struggle to use our public libraries is a tale that all should know. He would pretend to be asking for books for a white coworker and in this way continued to educate himself beyond "the scanty schooling the state furnished." The "bread of knowledge," Frederick Douglass called it, in his effort to learn to read and write, against all odds, however he could, whether by making poor white urchins his teachers or by reading and writing the letters marked on ship timbers in the shipyard where he worked.

During the Second World War, in that part of the world—Eastern Europe—where my family came from, a group, which came to be known as "The Paper Brigade," was formed that attempted to hide thousands of books and tens of thousands of documents from destruction by the Nazis, burying them in the ground, or in bunkers or attics, risking their lives daily by carrying them on their persons into the ghetto. Some thought them to be lunatic: while others were attempting to "smuggle foodstuffs into the ghetto, in their clothing and boots . . . [they] were smuggling books, pieces of papers." How could such a group occupy itself "with the fate of papers in such a time of crisis?" One member, Abraham Sutzkever, a poet, while "running through the streets of the ghetto with the pieces of parchment and poetry heard the words cry out to him: 'Hide me in your labyrinth.' Once, while burying the materials in the ground, he was overcome with despair. He then recalled an ancient parable: One of the Egyptian Pharaohs built a pyramid for himself, and ordered his servants to place some grains of wheat in his coffin at the time of his burial. Nine thousand years passed, the coffin was opened, the grains were discovered, planted, and a beautiful bed of stalks blossomed forth from them. Someday, Sutzkever wrote, the grains he was planting in the soil of the Vilna Ghetto would also bear fruit."

I remember clearly the day I was permitted to have my first library card. It was as if I had been granted full citizenship in this nation; it was that important. Entitlement to wander about among the stories of the world, to see places and people that never in my life could I have known about otherwise, to find models for a life ahead of me. I loved to read biographies of scientists, though in those days there were few women to read about. Madame Curie had a number of readings to compensate for the lack.

We are here to honor and celebrate our library's rededication, to thank those who labor in the vineyard of education, those who have had of late to reckon with one of the great revolutions—the advent of the computer. Truly this is the eighth wonder of the world, even for those of us who still hunger for the book as a book. The American poet William Stafford could walk through the stacks of a library, pick out a book, and tell within a decade the age of a book by the way it smelled.

We thank all including those most polite young people at the return desk who gently remind us when our books are overdue—all who work so well to make this library a living institution that benefits generations.

INTERVIEW WITH JOSEPH BRODSKY

February 28, 1979

In 1964 Joseph Brodsky was charged with social parasitism and convicted of idleness, a legitimate crime in the Soviet Union. He was sentenced to five years' hard labor in the Arkhangelsk region of Northern Russia. He speaks of this time in his life as a "previous incarnation." After pressure from many fronts, Brodsky was released having served twenty months of his sentence. In 1972 he came to America, to the University of Michigan, where a position had been arranged for him with the help of W. H. Auden and others. He had been befriended by the poet Anna Akhmatova during the last five years of her life. She considered Brodsky the most gifted lyric poet of his generation.

Brodsky came to Washington during the week of February 25, 1979 to take part in the International Symposium on Literary Translation and Ethnic Community run by the Department of Comparative Literature at the University of Maryland. Brodsky's works in English at that time included: Joseph Brodsky, Selected Poems, *translated by George Kline,* Gorbunov and Gorchakov, *and* A Part of Speech, *translated by Daniel*

Joseph Brodsky in late 1978 in front of his Greenwich Village apartment.
Photographer: Marianna Volkov.

Weissbort, forthcoming. He has translated many works from English into Russian, including the poetry of the English metaphysical poets. His technique for teaching himself English was to make literal translations of the first and last stanzas of the poetry of Auden, Yeats, Dylan Thomas, Eliot, and Wallace Stevens and then to "imagine" what should come in between.

We are in a Chinese restaurant—Arnost Lustig, the Czech novelist and short story writer; Brodsky's friend John Francis; and Cynthia Porter, a student who has spent some time in the Soviet Union. Brodsky orders for us all in a style reminiscent of a pasha ordering for his court. Squab, he announces. And shrimp. And dumplings, he says emphatically. No dumplings. For a moment I fear we will have to move again. This is the second restaurant we have tried, Brodsky having rejected the first. But I see that he is going to make do. The squab arrives, a plate of tiny elbows and knees.

MS: The last place I left off with you was in the sixties during the trial with the lady judge.

JB: That was in the previous incarnation almost.

MS: She asked you: "Who included you among the ranks of the poets?" And you said: "Who included me among the ranks of the human race?"

JB: That's right. Yah. Well, actually that was a (laughs) good comment on my part, although quite innocently.

MS: And then what did she say?

JB: I think . . . the way I remember, the most immediate line—I don't really remember that dialogue. In Russian you don't proceed in this kind of a way. Question, answer, logical development. No. No. So consequently you are not proceeding in this fashion, even if it is a dissident line delivered in public, it is not necessarily followed with a rebuttal.

MS: The poem that I love, "Gorbunov and Gorchakov . . ."

JB: Gorchakov [he offers, rolling the *r*. Brodsky's characters in this long poem are named Gorbunov, suggesting the word for hunchback, a kind of spiritual cripple, and Gorchakov, suggesting the Russian word for bitterness, a character who is himself embittered and who embitters the lives of others.]

MS: Is the whole work to be translated?

JB: It is. It does exist from cover to cover. It's by Ardis. The translation is rather informative. It informs you of what's going on. It has its own merit.

MS: Who did the translation?

JB: Mr. Carl Proffer. Well, he's running Ardis Publishing House and it's the first issue of *Russian Literature Triquarterly* . . . How do you like squabs, John?

JF: I haven't tasted them yet.

MS: Is *Metropol* going to happen?

JB: Yes. It's going to happen, by the same publishing house, Ardis. I don't know much about it. I've read only poems by one person there, a friend of mine . . . (Discussion of this project is not included here in deference to the wishes of Mr. Brodsky.) Publishing is a political thing, yah?

MS: I don't want to talk about political things. I want . . .

JB: Why not?

MS: I want to talk about your poetry.

JB: Oh well, it's better to talk politics.

MS: Yes, with poetry it's better to simply read the poetry. What do you think about the translation of Kline in this book (*Selected Poems*)?

JB: They're pretty good. Well . . . you should take into account . . . well they're good. I am luckier in English than nearly anybody, any Russian poet.

MS: Why?

JB: Well, because Kline is a serious man. He's quite a serious man, he's not a poet, so consequently it wasn't an ego trip on his part. He's a professor of history . . . philosophy. So he was trying to do an accurate job. Well, others are awfully lucky being translated by luminaries. Yah, well . . .

MS: Those translations worked well . . . except you never can tell how much . . . people like Robert Bly took great liberties; others stay closer to the text. The Hayward translations of Voznesensky's poetry always seemed so flat to me.

JB: So Voznesensky was luckier than me in one respect. Auden did one or two of his poems, which are much better in English in my view than in the original.

MS: But Auden wrote you a preface!

JB: I shouldn't complain.

MS: How did that relationship begin, yours with the work of Auden?

JB: Now I am going to tell you a story . . . When I got released in 1965, a friend of mine—he is still in Moscow, he's a translator of English and American poetry into Russian and he's a genius in my view and his judgment I used to trust more than anyone else's. And at one point he said about one of my poems, "Well it reminds me a great deal of Auden." Being compared to any English-speaking author was to me back then quite a compliment. I knew the man wouldn't fool with this parallel so I wanted to see what he was talking about.

My English at that time in 1965 . . . well, it's not perfect now, but if you can imagine . . . Well, anyway, I had begun to read Auden's poetry. I liked it a great deal because of its wit. I realized that this friend of mine wasn't exactly correct, though it was true with respect to that particular poem. At any rate I began to read Auden quite extensively, Auden and other people, but Auden in the first place because one thing which his poetry has, the bulk of Russian writing is lacking, a kind of detached, roundabout way, symptomatic technique. He is not talking about the ulcer itself. He is talking about its symptoms. That in itself is endearing.

I liked the face of the man, the photographs. I didn't know anything about him, not about his being a homosexual, or anything. At that point, if I had known, it would have mattered. Now, it doesn't. I loved the face, he has a great face. Actually, there are two faces I would rather have than my own, either his or Beckett's.

MS: I would like his bicycle and his face (Beckett's).

JB: Bicycle! Yah, well no. I would like his writing and his face. But well, the writing is quite impossible [Brodsky's long poem mentioned earlier, "Gorbunov and Gorchakov" has been compared with Beckett's *Waiting for Godot*.]

MS: Do you know the little one called *Play*?

JB: Yes I do. But the main thing, my affair started with Beckett and ended up . . . no, well not ended, it's still on . . . with *Malone Dies* and one of the loveliest things is the Dantean love story. You know it? Yah? . . . ["Dante and the Lobster"] And then I sent Auden some kind of Christmas postcard in that English . . . And here it was a year or two later a couple of people who were his New York friends came to Leningrad, a couple of Americans. I remember a terrible morning, headache and everything, you know, a Russian morning . . . something like eight o'clock . . . no I am lying . . . eight-thirty or nine, those people apparently had their breakfast in the restaurant. They walked, they found this address and the doorbell rang and two men popped up on my threshold, two impeccably dressed men, whereas I was trying to cover my whatever . . . frail and fairly naked body and there also was a terrible smell in the room, as there is after a man has been sleeping after a night . . . and that was in the winter I think. I remember I was trying to entertain them with some witty line or another and the coffee. Well, they brought my books and some greetings from him—Auden—and I again wrote to him. That was about it until 1972. There was one scholar who was in Austria during a conference and he brought regards to me, had guts enough to do it, from Wystan. So in 1972 . . .

MS: Was it dangerous to do that?

JB: It's always dangerous. Well, because it was after 1968 and Auden was not exactly the favorite person in the Soviet eyes because he had written that eight-liner about the invasion of Czechoslovakia. Whether you know it or not, it's a terrific poem: "The ogre does what the ogre can, something impossible to man . . ."

I knew that Auden spent summers in Austria so when I landed there, I asked a friend of mine from Michigan who came to meet me, whether we could try to trace Auden. We got a map of Austria, an Avis Volkswagen, and went there to comb the country. Well, there were three Kirchstetten in northern Austria . . . Finally we found what we were looking for and we came there and he was just returning from the terrain. We came to an empty house. Except for the woman cleaning, the woman in charge, there was nobody and then I see a figure climbing the hill in a red shirt and suspenders and gray jacket and books under his arm, sweating, and that was him.

I was staying in Austria for about two weeks and all the telegrams were coming to me from various places via him, well just out of the blue . . . well, I didn't really know from where. Also he was trying to direct my affairs and he did it quite a bit . . . well, he told me who to contact and who to deal with and also he squeezed out $1,000 from the Academy of American Poets, which was very essential at that point.

MS: To go back for a moment. You started looking at Auden's work after your friend told you that your work was similar?

JB: Yes, I had been doing that. I was reading English. It was a physical job [motions with his hands to indicate a huge dictionary] and I was just going word by word. But getting back to Auden, there is his poem in memory of Yeats and I showed it to my friend who was visiting me there, that poem, and especially the third part of it. He said, "Isn't it possible that they are writing better than us?" I said, "Well, looks like it." [laughs] Then what happened is that T. S. Eliot died January 1965 and I decided to write a poem and I took Auden's nearly for a model, though there are some variations, some fluctuations. Eliot was a great man. He was a great poet. Well, Cyril Connolly said that Auden was the last whose poems the English memorized. There is no way to memorize Eliot, I think.

MS: What was it like to finally meet Auden after that long-distance relationship?

JB: I don't know. He was, and this is the main thing about him, he was so humble, much more humble than Eliot, I would imagine, both as a man and as a poet. Whatever awe I felt was fading quite rapidly, not that it faded, but what was responsible for that awe, frankly, was not only Auden's performance, so to speak, but my inability to speak English.

MS: I was thinking of it the other way around too, what it was like for him to meet you?

JB: That I wouldn't know. . . . Except I hope I didn't irritate him much. Honestly.

AL: But it's so interesting, my God! First time that I saw Brodsky he was so sad. He came two years later than I did. When I saw him in Iowa City I understood it because I saw myself, so I told my friends, don't talk to him because he is sad, he is not interested in anything at all. He's simply sad. . . .

JB: Well, I don't know . . .

AL: We had this dinner. I had this feeling because I remembered how I felt two years before when I first came, because in Iowa we had the best time. They treated us like kings, they paid us . . .

JB: Not like kings . . .

AL: In Iowa they gave us $5,000 for eight months, a house in which I had never before lived, a beautiful white house [Paul Engel, the International Writing Program in Iowa] and I didn't enjoy it though every day was a party. And I thought, my God, I am really a sinner because everything is objectively so beautiful and I wasn't able to enjoy it because I would prefer to be in a suburb of Prague . . . and then came Brodsky and everyone asked why is he so sad and he was very shy and he didn't talk to many people and he came as a famous man and so everyone expected him . . .

JB: Squab! [Brodsky, in an effort to put an end to this part of the conversation piles Arnost's plate high with squab.] I will give you a squab. [Laughter]

AL: And then he came and didn't seem very pleased. So I told them, such is life. He is simply sad. We had a dinner and you were simply silent through the whole dinner.

JB: Could be. I don't really remember, 1974, I think.

AL: And you know, this was what nobody understood. Those others were strangers but they were so happy because they took the best of the United States and then left. And here was a Hungarian who said it openly. He was the son of a famous father. His father was a very great humorist in Budapest. And he was the only one who said: "Look, I am here for six months. I am trying to get the best. I know I am not going to stay here. I am going back," and it made him so happy that he could go back while looking at us that he really enjoyed it twice.

MS: What about that business of going back and not going back? . . . The impulse comes when one is at home in one's own landscape— or at least many people feel that way.

JB: I don't really know. Actually the best of it has been written outside of homes. Well, you think of Ovid and Dante.

MS: And Joyce.

JB: Eliot, if you wish. It's not exactly out of home. It's out of Missouri!

MS: Dante, did he return? Did he die in exile?

JB: No, he never returned. He died in Ravenna.

MS: And Ovid?

JB: Ovid, he died in Tomi, which is Rumania today, well not Rumania, Russia. Who else? But there were others. . . . Basically it's a difficult undertaking anyway. Either way it's difficult. It's bound to grow more difficult at any rate, whether you are at home or abroad. It's something else. No. It's a kind of scenario of difficulty. But on the other hand that's the real meaning of progress when things get more complicated. If you can manage, well, you can.

. . .

MS: Of the Russian poetry that I know, contemporary Russian poetry, that attitude of being in charge of one's country, of large matters, is more common than in this country, for example. Merwin is perhaps the extreme example of the writer of the inspection of stones, the poetry thinned out until finally it disappears. He has been very influential for younger poets. I suppose it is simply in the tradition of Russian writers to be on a much grander scale, to use everything . . .

JB: It's partly that, but partly the country is awfully centralized, so consequently the mentality of everybody is centralized in its own terms. It kind of reflects this centralization. For instance, we don't buy that much the notion of the subconscious. Yah. We think that the mind, the conscious is in charge of nearly everything. You report to your conscious mind all your instincts and emotions. This is one thing. Also, when you have such a centralization, when you have a centralized press, censorship, it turns the nation into a readership. Yah? So consequently you are addressing, willy nilly, you are addressing the nation.

MS: Does that then make the writer feel more responsible in a certain way? In America, when you write a poem, not many will read it. One is free to say almost anything.

JB: You just don't know. Certainly there is no guarantee that it is going to be read. On the contrary, there could be a guarantee of the opposite.

I open a fortune cookie and read the message inside. Arnost Lustig reads it aloud: "Nobody tells all he knows." And that seemed a fitting place to conclude the interview.

The evening of the interview I go to hear Brodsky read his poetry entirely in Russian to a Russian audience. The work is met with some hostility by the audience. He intones as though he were reciting a litany. Next to me a woman who has kindly been translating the work of the poet who shares the platform with Brodsky, refused to translate Brodsky's poetry for me. "It is like throwing stones in a face," she tells me as he recites. But I hear from others a line or two and I remember lines I've read of his poetry. One poem says with terrible irony, "Without the furniture, a person cannot survive."

The Howard Poets in
Perspective

*S*amuel Allen (the poet Paul Vesey) said once that an entire
generation of poets had been passed over in terms of public re-
cognition largely because it had come into its own before the
Civil Rights movement had gathered sufficient momentum. Pub-
lishing was essentially closed to the African American poet in the
late 1950s. Some—like Gwendolyn Brooks—who were able to
publish with the white literary establishment, turned away from
that marketplace and supported the Black publishing scene by
working with Dudley Randall's Broadside Press or before that
was a possibility, by publishing themselves. Percy Johnston put
it this way: "After all, the publisher was the one who paid the
printer and we figured we could do that ourselves."

So *Dasein,* a handsome national quarterly of the arts, came
into being in 1961 at Howard University. *Dasein* was a ma-
gazine dedicated to publishing poetry, fiction, and drama of
established as well as unknown writers "who maintain highest
literary standards." Percy Johnston was the publisher; Walter
DeLegall, the editor; Michael Winston, the executive editor;
William White, the art editor; Sterling Brown, Arthur P. Davis,

Owen Dodson, and Eugene Holmes, members of the advisory board; and the contributing editors were Al Fraser, Oswald Govan, Lance Jeffers, Leroy Stone, and Joseph White. Glancing through nearly any anthology of contemporary poetry it is not likely you will find the names of Oswald Govan or Lance Jeffers or LeRoy Stone. You might find Sterling Brown and then, taking a broad skip, the works of Nikki Giovanni, Alice Walker, and those of a younger generation.

In 1963 an anthology containing the works of the Howard Poets was published called *Burning Spear* and included poems by Walt De-Legall, Alfred Fraser, Oswald Govan, Lance Jeffers, Percy Johnston, Nathan Richards, LeRoy Stone, and Joseph White.

It is widely accepted that in the early 1950s and 1960s there were two significant gatherings of African American writers. One, the Umbra group in New York City, which included Ishmael Reed; the other in Washington. The Howard poets did not constitute a school or specific movement; their writings differed greatly. That there was a special kind of vitality to the literary scene then, that men and women from various disciplines were active writers and served to stimulate one another and those around them, I doubt any of the group would deny. Perhaps one way to characterize this group, and only loosely at that, is by something Percy Johnston said recently. He noted that his generation of poets was more closely attached, more conversant with the generation preceding his own than the younger poets are to the Howard poets. This fact is too important and too complex to conjecture about here, but in a study of more depth it should be addressed.

In 1925 a Dutch woman named Rosey Pool discovered Countee Cullen while working on a paper on contemporary American poetry. This began her lifelong interest in the poetry of African Americans. Percy Johnston and Walter DeLegall told that Rosey Pool sang Negro spirituals during her imprisonment by the Nazis for her work in the Underground during the Second World War. She had been Anne Frank's teacher. She came to this country in 1959 on a Fulbright and lectured in some twenty-seven Black colleges and in churches throughout the South, reading the poetry of Blacks. *Beyond the Blues,* an anthology of African American poetry, resulted and was published in England in 1962 and translated into Dutch. I am reminded here of the particular irony: Samuel Allen's first published works appearing in *Presence Africaine* published by Richard Wright in Paris and the next works appearing in Heidelberg in 1956. *Beyond the Blues* contains works by some of the Howard poets.

Though not an exhaustive list of the Howard poets, I attempted to locate Lance Jeffers, Walter DeLegall, LeRoy Stone, Al Fraser, Clyde Taylor, David Dorsey, Joe White, Laura Watkins, Dolores Kendrick, and Oswald Govan. Edward Watson has come along, thanks to Percy, to join the group.

There were other writers here in Washington in the late 1950s. May Miller speaks of the group that met in a workshop which included Charles Sebrey the artist, Texeira Nash, Percy Johnston, Owen Dodson, Lance Jeffers, Toni Morrison, Charles Wilder, and Claude Brown. Brown was at work at that time on *Manchild in the Promised Land*.

And there was still another group called the Washington Poets that gave readings frequently at a place called Coffee and Confusion, which opened on April Fool's Day in 1959 around Washington Circle. It was closed after ten days and in June of the same year moved to Tenth and K, N.W. This group included Bill Walker, Dick Dabney, Percy Johnston, Bill Jackson, and Lester Blackiston.

Sterling Brown was then and continues to be a critically important influence for all writers through his writings, essays, and poetry, and through his fifty years of teaching as a primary intellectual and moral force.

Stephen Henderson in *Understanding the New Black Poetry*[11] says of the *Dasein* poets: "Their sense of history, their precise knowledge of the importance of Black culture, their absorption of modern scientific thought into the fabric of their poetry stands in contrast to the parochialism of some more recent writers. Although the influence of the Beat movement upon them is obvious, what is less obvious in the case of Percy Johnston, for example, is the way the *Dasein* poets embody and amplify the Black influence upon the Beat movement itself."

And Dolores Kendrick says: "The Movement you mentioned was, as I remember, the *Dasein* Group—a group of poets and prose writers assembled by Percy Johnston, who edited the magazine *Dasein* from Howard University. The group was unique in that the people involved were concerned about the skill and permanence of their art. Percy once explained to me, concerning this new Black image, that it, too, would pass and that when it did, the Black writers of substance and integrity would still be writing and celebrating their craft. I believe he was right."

Eugene Redmond, in his anthology *Drumvoices: A Critical History*, comes as close as anything I've read in accurately characterizing the Howard poets:

As a group the Howard Poets represent one of the toughest intellectual strains in contemporary Black poetry. Maybe the fact of their having such diverse interests, backgrounds and training aided in their vitality, virtuosity and power. To be sure, these are conscious poets, but—avoiding slogans and sentimental hero worship—they present precise analysis and interpretation of their world. Most of them grew up in the bebop era and so their subjects quite naturally include Miles Davis, Lester Young, Charlie Parker, Clifford Brown, Sonny Rollins, Thelonious Monk, and other makers and contributors of that period. A concern for civil rights and Black struggle merges with an awareness of "the bomb," of middle class pretensions, history, mythology, religion, and the various trends in poetry: modernity, Beat poetry, jazz and folk lyrics.[12]

This collection of poems, these words of introduction, do not begin to provide a sense of the Howard Poets, their range, intelligence, humor, sense of history. With each word written here, I hear the voice of one or another saying, "but you've got it all wrong. It was like this." In answer I can only say that this won't be an accurate history. That has to be written by the members of the group itself. Nobody else can do it. But that something important was happening then and continues to happen is undeniable. And the story will never be complete without knowing something of what these quite extraordinary men and women wrote, the poems that provide evidence and testimony of this generation of writers.[13]

COUNTERPOINT

*F*or ten years I have loved a poem, a small poem that I have never understood. I bring the poem to my classes year after year and read it aloud in English and then I find a student who is able to read it in the original Spanish for the class.

The student always begins, "Agosto, contraponientes de melocoton y azucar . . ." (August, the opposing of peach and sugar), and that is where the difficulty begins and seems to end. It is not hard to imagine what Federico Garcia Lorca had intended when he said "The sun inside of the afternoon like the stone in the fruit," nor "The ear of corn which keeps its laughter intact, yellow and firm." Nor even—to go to the end—"The little boys eat brown bread and rich moon." I do not know when he wrote the poem. I have always meant to look it up. Every now and then a curious student will bring us a fact or two about Lorca that I promptly forget, starting each semester over again with only the little poem for evidence.

Agosto . . .

Agosto,
contraponientes
de melocoton y azucar,
y el sol dentro de la tarde,
como el hueso en una fruta.

La panocho gaurda intacta
su risa amarilla y dura.

Agosto.
Los ninos comen
pan moreno y rica luna.[14]

August . . .

August,
the opposing
of peach and sugar,
and the sun inside of the afternoon
like the stone in the fruit.

The ear of corn keeps
its laughter intact, yellow and firm.

August.
The little boys eat
brown bread and rich moon.

When a student who sat quietly alert during the first class announces that he really won't be able to continue in your class because he has decided to enroll in Logic, you breathe deeply and compliment him on his choice. There is certainly no logic here.

Later, I thought about his voice, the careful way he moved, the brief-case he carried, the suit and short hair so out of keeping with the style of dress of the others, the face that could be seventeen or forty, the precision of speech, the look of someone who had not known many happy moments in his life, and I thought how glad I was to be done with him.

I thought fleetingly of my recent conclusion that it was absolutely impossible to determine at the outset who of a class of students would bring forth his own voice into the midst of the writing class, where he might then be hopelessly cut off by the others or where he might flourish, if indeed only for the length of one semester, thirty-seven hours, if he came on time. I went home to look over the questionnaires I had given them, which I knew they hated but provided me with the opportunity to watch them in the first few moments of the first class and, for those who finish questionnaires quickly, gave them a chance to watch me. I continue to watch them as I pass out pieces of paper filled with course requirements, poems, sections of prose, and work in other languages. I always explain that this is not my field, that I am a biologist, a physiologist, that I work with monkeys, Rhesus monkeys, that I do not know English and American literary history but do know a little about frontal lobe function of the brain and once studied perceptual losses (which outfits me perfectly for teaching, though I don't say that). In truth, that was years ago, but it seems to get me off the hook a bit—I am a writer, not a scholar—and then I can continue to pass out those ditto sheets covered with Lorca, Neruda (one semester my students seemed surprised, when Neruda won the Nobel Prize, that I hadn't invented the name!), Cortazar, Borges, pages filled with Greek prose poems of Sinopoulos, works of Poles, Italians, Russians, my hands turning purple. They smile sadly and accept, accept.

Later I warn them that I cannot bear poems about love and death—that to get to those subjects they must begin with stones, fingernails; that all things, no matter how abstract they have become, were once based on real events, real objects, real relationships. I tell them that the bodies in the Nile River, which the lad Ipu Wer speaks of 2,300 years before Christ, are as real as the bodies that flowed in the Mekong River in this century. I tell them that the wine cup, the vineyards Rilke speaks of as the lost objects are as real as the words we form to say their names.

In the next class he is back. His name is Bonfiglio. He has decided to take the course after all. But what has happened to Logic? His answer is the familiar yellow slip from the registrar's office thrust at me to sign, which of course I do. I always sign them.

I swing from branch to branch carrying them passively along with me while they have permission to poke and prod and make demands. I carry them along with me for years until they are ready to move on their own or until they have found someone else to take my place.

It seemed time to try out the poem on them. Each year I invent a new excuse for hauling it out. This semester we would observe the manner in which the writer entered the language. After all, was it not the beginning of a new semester? Is it not the issue of each new semester to begin? And, as Rilke tells us, is it not a tremendous act of violence to begin anything? He simply skips over what should be the beginning. He is not able to begin. For, he tells us, nothing is so powerful as silence. It would never have been broken had we not, each of us, been born into the midst of talk. The midst of talk—that seems to be what is expected in the classroom, though writers are peculiarly inarticulate. I certainly don't like to talk. I like to wait, to be silent, to watch. I should probably spend more time letting them write, fill up the seventy-five minutes (if we start on time) with the sound of their arms moving along the table, the black letters clouding over the pages like a storm.

The question is, What to do with Bonfiglio? In a poem I have been writing, which remains unfinished with all the others like limb buds that have never stretched out to become legs and arms, there is a line about a line that has traveled a great distance and when it returns it longs for those things it touched on its journey and could not or did not name. It is these things it remembers. That is my dilemma with Bonfiglio. I can neither give him up nor keep him. Soon enough he will disappear. I cannot rely on telling him as a story. It will grow thin and change. Someone will repeat my story to someone else and Bonfiglio will never be the same again. Each time I think of Bonfiglio he changes in my mind.

To go back or forward—it is no longer clear—we skirted the issue of those lines, agreeing that the Spanish was better, the lines flowed softly—*de melocoton*—how could one substitute the word *peach* for that mellifluous word that called up exotic landscapes, Greek apples, Spanish shrubs, skin pigment, melodies that sing at the very sound of the word as it moves away from the mouth. And wasn't *azucar* somehow more attractive than *sugar*—so American, so harsh, somehow embarrassing, like having a beloved relative suddenly emerge from the kitchen where she has spent her whole life, to appear framed in the doorway of one's adolescence into which she has just now escaped, now caught in the full glare of the first light of consciousness, that stunted and prejudiced consciousness given so casually to youngsters. But why peaches and sugar, which were opposing, which were the *contraponientes* of August?

At home the night before I had developed a theory that it was a poem of internalizations, great planetary forms taken in by microscopic bodies—the sun inside of the afternoon like the stone in the fruit, laughter within an ear of corn, bread and moon inside the little boys. In class, contributions came like small charities but the dissatisfaction remained. I gathered up the pages and said aloud that I did not think we had solved those first three lines and I looked ahead silently to new semesters where someone would come and magically unravel those simple words. I kept thinking of the Spanish word *contraponientes*—counterpoint. I thought of Bach. I imagined my fingers into the fugues and preludes, playing each line cleanly without weight or emphasis, so that each could be heard as purely as the other. I thought of Glenn Gould playing the same thing better on his harpsichord in the Canadian north woods. I thought how I had always wanted to write a poem whose structure was that of the fugue. The poet Zukofsky says that he has been doing just that for forty years. I just wanted to try it for a day or so, a little poem, but none ever came.

Without warning Bonfiglio began to speak, quietly, with great care and precision, exactly as one might have expected. "In certain countries," he began, "for example in Cuba, in parts of Italy and Spain, the harvest season for both peach and sugar occurs in August and one must make a judgment as to which shall be harvested first. Often it is determined that the peach will be gathered first because it is the more fragile. But great care must be taken to bring in both peach and sugar before the hail storms arrive. This is also the time of the festival of the harvest. The women make a good rich brown bread." In August I will go out under the rich moon to have a look for myself. Corn, peach, sugar, hail, and brown bread. Jon Bonfiglio has earned his place in the class if he never utters another word.

Life, The Unfinished Experiment

THE SELFISH GENE

(or, Cortazar's Watch)

In the world according to Argentine writer Julio Cortazar, when we are presented with a watch we are being gifted with "a tiny flowering hell, a wreath of roses, a dungeon of air." It is not simply a "good brand, Swiss, seventeen rubies," not a "minute stonecutter which will bind you by the wrist and walk along with you," but "the gift of fear" that "someone will steal it from you . . . they aren't giving you a watch, you are the gift, they're giving you yourself for the watch's birthday."[1]

In the gospel according to Richard Dawkins,[2] we are—as with Cortazar's watch—the gift that has been given for the gene's birthday. In this scenario we are, along with all organisms, plants as well as animals, essentially survival machines directed by the selfish genes. We are discarded like so much baggage once we have fulfilled our role as transitory site for the gene. We are so many rail cars, so much seawater, so long as we are essential for housing the gene and carrying out *its* instructions. What may appear as altruism in a given species is merely a tactic for enabling the gene to survive, and to do so more efficiently than another gene in another population. Our tendency to attribute values to certain forms of behavior—nonaggressive behavior is good; altruism is what we hope for, etc.—is not what the gene has in mind for us.

Dawkins postulates that a remarkable molecule formed by accident over hundreds of millions of years had the ability to act as template not for an identical copy but for "a kind of negative, which would in its turn re-make an exact copy of the original positive." Dawkins argues that Darwin's 'survival of the fittest' is actually an example of *survival of the stable,* which he defines by the length of time a molecule lasts, the ability to replicate rapidly, or the ability to replicate accurately. Since the primeval soup was not capable of supporting an infinite number of replicator molecules, *competition* is the second element at work here. These replicators, he tells us, go by the name of genes and we are their survival machines.

We are all survival machines for DNA molecules—monkeys for preserving genes up trees, fish to preserve genes in the water, "even a small worm which preserves genes in German beer mats," says Dawkins.

And what is the selfish gene? It is, according to Dawkins, not one physical bit of DNA but all replicas of that DNA distributed throughout the world.

Is there a counterpart to the replicator that has arisen from the soup of human culture? Dawkins calls it meme-tunes, ideas, catchphrases, methods of building arches. Memes propagate through imitation. As with high survival value in genes, memes must be capable of longevity, fecundity, and copying fidelity.

We *are* given a crumb of hope: "Selfish genes have no foresight," he concludes. "They are unconscious, blind replicators." Whereas we may "have the power to turn against our creators." There are ways that our selfish genes have been put to work for us. Viruses (little DNA packages in overcoats), acting as vectors—though safely modified to prevent full expression of their attributes in our bodies—can be made to transport genetic material or toxins, which will act on our behalf against pathogens in us, and in the long run will give us and our selfish genes a bit more time in this world.

THE KNOCKOUT MOUSE ON THE
DOORSTEP OF NEUROBIOLOGY
(or, the Mind/Body Problem
Revisited)

*T*hese days, neuroscience is beginning to resemble philosophy. The age-old questions about the nature and location of consciousness, the relationship of mind to body and self to physical world, are being asked once again, but this time in more concrete terms by neuroscientists.

Our concept of the relation between ourselves and the physical world is thought by Leif Finkel through his work on visual perception and computer modeling to be a representation of an internal construct that we project upon the external world. In his words, "much of the consistency and logic of external events is then a property of the 'perceiver' rather than the perceived object. . . . What we take to be the basic physical properties of our environment, may reflect the structure of our brains more than the structure of the universe."[3]

Perhaps Dante was considering the mind/body question with his emblematic use of Bertrand de Born—the troubadour who set father against son and walked the rim of the eighth circle of the Inferno carrying his severed head by the hair, swinging it like a lantern: "I bear my brain divided from its source within this trunk." We might also remember Jonathan Swift's interdigitation—the exchange of a half-brain of one leader with that of another to achieve a modicum of peace. Neither shed much light on the nature of reconciliation. However, both pointed to the possibility that the "human body and the human mind met inside the skull." We leave behind Aristotle who set mind farther down, in the rag and bone shop of the heart.

One most curious phenomenon on its way to being deciphered is exactly how developing neurons make connections with one another. Each nerve cell can form up to 10,000 such connections or synapses. Does the wiring plan call for a complete construction of all such connections? Or is the brain so adaptive, so flexible that its architecture involves a basic framework with the rest of the constructive work left to brain function itself?

As Dr. Carla Shatz, Chair, Department of Neurobiology, Harvard Medical School, describes it, "The wiring diagram of the adult brain is wonderfully complex and precise, as if nothing has been left to chance. How is this precision achieved during brain development? . . . It is not as easy as soldering together the connections of a computer." Axons must recognize their correct targets and must bypass other areas, "just as [we] might drive past Philadelphia en route from New York to Washington."[4]

Dr. Shatz tells us that "there are really two broad phases to brain wiring: an early phase that lays down basic brain circuits and does not require brain activity, and a later phase that refines circuits into their adult precision" through brain activity. An elegant illustration of this two-phase process occurs with the circuitry to do with language. The brain doesn't know if its owner will speak English or Serbo-Croatian. Thus, the fundamental framework is laid down and is, in theory, applicable to all languages. The specifics of a particular language are not brought into play until after the birth of the child. Thus the exquisitely adaptive relation between self and environment.

Understanding neuronal development may prove useful in the eventual treatment of neurological diseases and trauma. The ability to regenerate nerve cells is of considerable clinical importance. How can nerve cell growth and survival be facilitated? Nerve cells in culture have not provided the answers. But a learned borrowing from a companion science, immunology, the use of so-called knockout mice (mice that have been genetically altered) has recently penetrated the field of neurobiology. Previous studies were done with the use of antibodies that interfered with nerve growth factors. But the application of the first animal model lacking one of the four known neurotrophin molecules (neurotrophins promote survival and differentiation of various nerve cell populations) has the potential of advancing our understanding of neuronal development and hence our ability to evaluate potential treatment for human neurological diseases.

The ultimate goal is to understand how different neurotrophins interact during neural development to produce an intact embryo, and then learn to recreate these interactions to heal or rescue damaged nerve cells later in life.

"It is understandable," says Gustav Eckstein, "that Nature built such a stockade around that precious flesh [our brains], bone that is light but strong and shaped into a form that has elicited the admiration of architect and engineer."[5] And it is entirely possible that a small mouse may help to solve some of the mysteries embodied in that globe we carry about on our shoulders, a few pounds—give or take—capable of dreaming, inventing, capable of motion, even able to comprehend itself.

AIDS: LATENCY AND
HIV RESERVOIRS
In the Dark Backward
and Abysm of Time

*P*rospero, in Shakespeare's *The Tempest,* inquires of his daughter Miranda what she remembers of her hidden past: "What seest thou else/ In the dark backward and abysm of time?" Thus does Prospero proceed to fill in the silence, telling how they came to reside on an island, of twelve years lived in an apparent time-out from the ways of the world and the conspiratorial nature of its inhabitants.

Shakespeare's metaphor for latency has its counterparts in all of nature. We speak in botanical terms of buds whose flowers are not yet manifest, or in embryology of the limb buds that will give way to our arms and legs. We speak of hidden character, of dormancy, of latent energy potential; in disease, of the incubation period between initial exposure and expression of symptoms; in psychological terms of that swinging bridge (called the latency period) between temporary resolution of the oedipal struggles and the onset of puberty, a time of immense cognitive development in children.

So with AIDS, it had been thought that the human immunodeficiency virus entered a state of latency that accounted for up to a decade of subclinical infection in some patients and that it was through later activation of the virus that acute disease processes became manifest. But what, in fact, had been going on during the apparent quiescence of the virus? Had HIV been incorporated into the host genome and independent replication ceased? To all intents and purposes the virus disappeared from peripheral T cells.

It was not difficult to measure the presence of the HIV virus in the blood, but far more difficult to detect its presence in the lymph tissue. It turns out that ninety-eight percent of the virus is harbored there, and it now appears that the establishment of the virus in the lymph tissue occurs early in the course of the disease, even if treatment with a four-drug combination including a protease inhibitor is begun early. At the World AIDS Conference in 1998, Dr. Anthony Fauci, director of the National Institute of Allergy and Infectious Diseases at the National Institutes of Health, discussed the importance of diminishing these latent pools of HIV virus, of finding ways to flush out the virus in lymph tissue. The knowledge of HIV latency offers an understanding for why, when multiple-drug therapies are withdrawn, the "rebound" effect of the virus is so rapid and so potent.

Therapeutic strategies must take into account this reservoir of protein-coated virus present in the lymph nodes and the potential of this virus to infect circulating CD4+ T cells. The effective duration of drugs used to inhibit or disrupt portions of the life cycle of the virus is one factor. Immune therapies must target viral complexes on follicular dendritic cells in lymph tissue without causing the cells to become infected. The case for early intervention seems more pointed here in delaying a firm foothold by the virus in the lymphoid tissues.

As in Prospero's seeming reprieve from the world in *The Tempest,* the latency period in HIV infection is anything but quiescent. From the virus's point of view there is much work to be done. If we are essential survival machines directed by the selfish genes, as Richard Dawkins would have it, necessary for housing a virus and carrying out its instructions in the case of HIV, perhaps the virus has outsmarted itself, for in the act of finishing us off, it has done itself in as well. True, the reader might argue, but the virus survives quite well in the large pool of those afflicted. On the other hand, we might just find a way to put the virus to work for us, as vehicle for redirecting our genetic machinery in useful and unforseen ways.

HUMAN GENE THERAPY

Harnessing the Body's
Defenses Against Cancer

*S*cientists, like Talmudic scholars, work along a continuum—some researching the minute particulars of an issue, others looking at whole structures. The Talmudist might ask: How shall we know which prayers to recite during the three watches of the night? By what signals shall we determine when the watch has concluded and a new one begun? And what guide shall inform us of the arrival of morning? Some say, when you can tell the difference between a white thread and a blue. Or when you can distinguish between a wolf and a dog. Others in this tradition engage in debate over more comprehensive issues and devote their lives to considering major ethical or legal systems.

Dr. Steven Rosenberg, chief of surgery at the National Cancer Institute, belongs in this second category, attempting to address the way the body itself reveals its own strategies for maintaining its integrity and health and provides a complex surveillance system to do so. By harnessing the body's own defense system, augmenting it, amplifying the body's ability to *recognize* foreign cells and deal appropriately with them, rather than seeking to use agents external to the body, Rosenberg takes part in a new chapter in biologic therapies and cancer treatment. Chemotherapy, radiation and surgery aim directly at the cancer. Biologic therapy assists the body in recognizing and responding to cancer-causing agents.

CANCER INCIDENCE: Why be concerned with developing new weapons against cancer? Chemotherapy, surgery, and radiation have provided a fifty percent cure rate in terms of normal actuarial survival. Rosenberg is quick to point out that despite the improvement in survival, the incidence of cancer is staggering. In 1991 deaths from cancer in the United States numbered 515,000. Compared with 300,000, the total of all deaths in World War II: 57,000 deaths in Viet Nam: 18,000 deaths last year from AIDS, it would not seem that we have come very far in our efforts to slow down the effects of cancer. One out of four people now alive will develop invasive cancer.

BIOLOGIC THERAPY—WHAT IS IT? In biologic therapy an attack is not mounted against the cancer directly as it is with chemotherapy, surgery, and radiation. The body recognizes some cancers as foreign but at times it is a weak recognition. Therefore the body's defense against cancer must be altered. The host is assisted in its ability to fight by enlisting the cellular arm of the immune system. The question is, How can the body's immune response be stimulated?

There were known albeit rare instances of spontaneous regressions of cancers. Could these provide any clues to strategies for treatment? Twenty-three years ago Rosenberg, then in surgical training, treated such a patient who some twelve years earlier had been diagnosed with a metastatic, essentially untreatable stomach tumor. To Rosenberg's surprise, the patient was alive and well all these years later. Could the use of this man's cells shed any light on cancer treatment? Efforts to treat both humans and animals, including an attempt to grow a sarcoma nodule in the mesentery of miniature pigs and transfuse treated cells by IV back to a patient, were unsuccessful.

One of the missing ingredients in those days was some way to grow lymphocytes outside of the body and to amplify them. Robert Gallo's group at NIH provided the key through the isolation of a T-cell hormone, Interleukin-2.

THE ARSENAL: The body's ability to react immunologically to tumor cells can be inhibited in at least two of the following ways: tumor-killing cells can have difficulty reading the tumor cells as foreign; if the recognition function does work effectively, the immunological response can sometimes mobilize not only the killer cells but also the suppressor cells whose function it is to regulate the immune response.

Knowledge of four key substances produced by the body—interleukin-2 (IL-2), tumor-necrosing factor (TNF), lymphokine-activated killer cells (LAK), tumor infiltrating lymphocytes (TIL)—has opened the way to current research. IL-2, interleukin-2, is a T-lymphocyte growth factor that both increases the number of T-lymphocytes and activates certain T-cells to become cancer-killing cells called lymphokine-activated killer cells or LAK. These killer cells cause no harm in vitro to normal cells, a great advantage over chemotherapy, which is indiscriminate in its harm to both normal and malignant cells.

Several curious observations about these LAK cells: they have no antigen receptors so that recognition is nonspecific. They recognize any change on the cell surface and are thought to be part of a very primitive surveillance system. If the cell surface is modified in any way, LAK cells are poised to kill. In normal cells, the cell membrane protects against LAK cells. LAK cells will die in less than a day in the absence of IL-2.

TIL, tumor-infiltrating lymphocyte, is both vector and cancer killing and acts in a very specific way. It has the precise ability to recognize a specific tumor and metastatic tumors at quite distant sites. Therefore TIL targets the tumor and distant associated tumors. When TIL is used with tumor-necrosing factor (TNF), it minimizes the toxicity of TNF to the rest of the body and maximizes TNF's benefit, that of cutting off the developing blood supply to the tumor.

TNF was first observed during bacterial infections and appears to have a regulatory function, its powerful effect against tumors an apparent side effect of its main function.

STAGING: One of the first difficulties to overcome was to demonstrate the feasibility and safety of using a modified retrovirus derived from a mouse leukemia retrovirus. Was there any danger of this retrovirus randomly integrating a new gene into the human genome? Extensive studies were done in vitro prior to studies using human TIL. In both cases it was established that the properties of human TIL were not altered, that these procedures could be performed with little risk to the patient and none to health-care personnel.

Why use leukemia retroviruses in the first place? Because of the high efficiency of gene transfer using this technique. Rosenberg points out that the retroviruses used are not capable of replication, and that in any case, genes are not being introduced into the germline but into somatic cells.

Current treatment is with melanoma patients. "Our goal is to put a little crack in the granite face of melanoma," says Rosenberg. There is currently no cure for melanoma and those treated are in the terminal stages of their disease. "We would be happy to treat patients whose disease is much less advanced." Rosenberg refers to the brief window of time—less than ninety days—there is for treatment and the extreme difficulty of rallying the body's immune defenses at this late stage.

Once the safety issues passed review by a series of oversight committees, treatment was begun in the following way: A small section of a patient's tumor was surgically removed. A retrovirus derived from a mouse leukemia retrovirus was modified through recombinant DNA technology to transport the gene for TNF into the tissue. This mixture was then injected into the patient's thigh. After an interval of three weeks, lymph nodes in this region were removed to obtain those lymphocytes particularly active against the tumor. These white cells were then cultured and amplified in the laboratory and returned to the patient, the genetic priming of the tumor cells aimed at producing large quantities of TNF, which enhances recognition and furthers tumor destruction.

A second strategy involved inserting the gene for TNF into tumor-infiltrating lymphocytes from a melanoma patient's tumor. It was found, by radioactive labeling of tumor-infiltrating lymphocytes—that TIL destroyed tumor cells by direct contact and by stimulating products of other substances capable of killing tumor cells. A benefit of using TIL with IL-2 is that far less IL-2 is required, thus reducing the extreme toxicity caused by IL-2 to kidneys and liver because of water retention.

Human trials continue; the results are not all in. It is difficult to know, when one stands in the midst of scientific work, what its true significance is. Just as it took half a century to understand the significance of Peyton Rous's work in 1911, causing sarcomas to develop in newly hatched chicks by injecting cell-free filtrates of large chicken sarcomas. Viruses could not then be seen through a microscope.

It is clear that a scientific revolution is taking place. Never has communication in science been more far-reaching. Researchers working in Sweden are in touch with their counterparts in the United States, in

Tokyo, in Africa. And unlike the past, where treatments were sometimes found without understanding disease cause, with the advent of biologic therapies we have come to a time of increasing knowledge of the body's own strategies for living in a dynamic equilibrium with other living systems. The general pool of knowledge has expanded at a geometric rate greatly augmenting the kinds of investigations that are possible. Even as these melanoma trials go on at the National Cancer Institute, a team of researchers in Brussels adds a new piece of information to the structure of the whole: They have discovered an antigen on tumor cells taken from people with malignant melanoma that serves as a signal to stimulate cancer-fighting cells. They have identified the gene that codes for this protein as well.

At NIH, Steve Rosenberg, more Akiba—the first-century codifier of Talmudic Oral Law—than Eliezer—a thirteenth-century commentator—approaches the human citadel and dares, like the good surgeon he is, to make inroads in our knowledge of the cellular basis of immunity. As with the breaking of any taboo, such work will not always be greeted with equanimity. There are those who object to man's tampering with the human genome. Though Rosenberg takes quite seriously concerns about ethics, religion, and safety, he reflects wistfully that very likely "the first person to open an umbrella was told: God meant for us to get wet." As for the apprehension of the particular as opposed to the comprehensive, as with the Talmud, in science both are absolutely essential modes of exploration.[6]

THE PUZZLE PEOPLE

"*A*t a meeting in Capri not long ago," Thomas Starzl writes in his *Memoirs,* "I was asked by an Italian journalist, 'Do you think that in the next decade a puzzle man with a heart, liver and pancreas taken from other human beings might be feasible?'" Starzl, an international pioneer in the controversial field of transplant surgery, characterized by colleague Samuel Wells as one who has made a "contribution of such magnitude and significance that it clearly represents a new direction in that field," lingered over the journalist's question. The conservation of life, whether at the molecular level or at the level of organ systems, involved "not just the acquisition of a new part; the rest of the body had to change . . . before the gift could be accepted." Starzl points out that "patients were not the only puzzle people . . . being forged." Physicians too underwent change because "the lives of others were in their hands."

The notion of the puzzle people would prove to be prophetic. Starzl recently confirmed what had earlier been circumstantial, the discovery that donor recipients like the mythical chimera—part lion, goat, and serpent—contain not only the donated organ. Through new DNA fingerprinting techniques it was discovered that genetic material from the transplanted organ had migrated throughout the body of the recipient to blood, lymph nodes, and skin, offering the future possibility of reducing the need for antirejection medications, which leave the body open to infection.

In an effort to search out the "riddle of striving," Starzl tells his own story beginning with his childhood in LeMars, Iowa. At his family's newspaper where he worked as a youngster, he observed the manual dexterity of the printers. "If in the 1930s I wanted to teach a class of surgeons economy and precision of movement, the print shop of a small town in Iowa would have been a good place to start." Another surgeon's lesson can be found in Dr. Starzl's description of his father's "love of translating ideas into real structure," inventions including photoelectric engraving and an oxygenator his father made from a farmer's cream can.

As in the writings of other physician/researchers—George Klein in *The Atheist and the Holy City*, Francois Jacob in *The Statue Within*— Starzl's *Memoirs*[7] provides a context for the thrust of his life in transplant research and the path he forged. The book is part autobiography, part documentary in its tracings of the journey of transplantation research, its major players and research centers, Starzl's particular mentors, the legal and ethical issues that pertained in this thirty-five-year enterprise. A Latin scholar who had once considered the priesthood, Thomas Starzl, armed with a medical degree from Northwestern and a doctorate in neurophysiology, joined the surgical training program at Johns Hopkins, which had boasted the likes of Harvey Cushing and was headed by Dr. Alfred Blalock.

In 1962, Dr. Starzl began his pioneering research in kidney transplant surgery at the University of Colorado. Better antirejection therapy, improved means of organ procurement and preservation, the efficacy of tissue typing—a host of issues had to be resolved. Starzl performed human kidney transplantation on an identical twin, circumventing the problem of rejection. The recipient was still alive twenty-nine years later. That same year, Dr. Starzl, using a combination of irradiation and steroids to combat rejection, performed a kidney transplant using a nonidentical donor. It seemed a major obstacle had been removed. The patient returned to school several weeks later. The eventual goal—liver transplantation—would have to wait until better methods of immunosuppression could be found.

As Lewis Thomas wrote in *Lives of a Cell*, if he were told that he was now in charge of his liver, he'd rather take the controls of a 747 jet 40,000 feet over Denver. "I am considerably less intelligent than my liver." "What," asks Richard Selzer in *Mortal Lessons*, "is the size of a pumpernickel, has the shape of Diana's helmut, and crouches like a thundercloud above its bellymates? What has the industry of an insect, the regenerative powers of a starfish, yet is turned to a mass of fatty globules by a double martini?" The liver: largest organ of our body. A massive chemistry of innumerable reactions streams in that stew kettle, Gustav Eckstein tells us. The liver can rebuild to its old contours. Detoxify. Synthesize amino acids. Produce bile. Though it is a single organ, no mate, it is composed of many factories. Like a huge century plant after its ultimate bloom, it makes a noisy death. Imagine then the difficulty of replacing it. For Starzl, "the road to the liver would have to lead through the kidney."

The first human liver transplant was performed on a three-year-old child who lacked the tubular duct system that collects bile, a condition known as biliary atresia. The operation could not be completed; the failure of his blood to clot and scarring caused by the liver's efforts to repair itself resulted in hemorrhaging and death. Since that first attempt, Starzl has performed more than 3,600 liver transplants, opening the way for this procedure to become common practice; some 20,000 in all have been performed. Since 1981, Starzl has been at the University of Pittsburgh where earlier this year the first animal-to-human liver transplant was done. Who could have predicted that experimental liver replacement surgery in animals in the 1950s, a "solitary dot on a nearly empty canvas," would result in a procedure performed in medical centers around the world?

The same restless energy that moves between Starzl's childhood in Iowa and his work in surgery in this memoir is the engine that drives his continued pioneering work. In *The Puzzle People*, Thomas Starzl grapples with integrating the various aspects of his life: childhood and the rites of passage that took a young man who was like a "missile looking for a trajectory" to his chosen work.

Genes, Blood, and Courage

A Boy Called Immortal Sword

*T*he question arises in these decades of radical change in science and medicine: Who shall tell the stories of medical quests and scientific discoveries? More often now the stories are being told by the researchers and physicians at the center of discovery. Some are told as memoirs—as with François Jacob's *The Statue Within* or Salvador Luria's *A Slot Machine, A Broken Test Tube;* some as medical or scientific detective stories as in *The Double Helix* by James Watson or *Bright Air, Brilliant Fire: On the Matter of Mind* by Gerald Edelman. Still others provide a view from the greater distance as in Luria's *Life—The Unfinished Experiment* or Peter Medawar's *The Threat and the Glory.*

In a sense, David Nathan's *Genes, Blood, and Courage*[8] embodies each of these approaches and is a hybrid—part medical detective story, part philosophy, part human narrative, part memoir. The work sets us to ruminating about the evolution of three-and-a-half billion years of life on our planet—on natural selection and its ability to subtract, on mutation and its ability to add. As Lewis Thomas wrote in *The Medusa and the Snail:* "The capacity to blunder slightly is the real marvel of DNA.

Without this special attribute, we would still be anaerobic bacteria and there would be no music."

At the same time, this complex work is built upon a beautiful, elucidating narrative structure—the story of a child with thalassemia whose experiences we will follow through twenty-seven years of treatment, through the transforming work of molecular biology and genetics that has come to inform the practice of medicine in new and extraordinary ways today. This narrative, like the shape of the double helix—the spiral backbone of DNA—provides the structure for the scientific and ethical debates of our time. And we learn about the development of techniques that will change the face and shape of treatment for thalassemia permanently and worldwide.

The book commences with an unlikely pairing: a genetic adaptation destructive of its host on the one hand, where nucleated immature red blood cells arrive in the bloodstream unable to fully oxygenate the body's tissues, yet where the presence of the gene for thalassemia is protective of its bearer against malaria. Thus, in regions of the world where malaria is endemic, the incidence of thalassemia is disproportionately high. Thalassemia derives its name from the Greek word for sea, θαλασσα (Thalassa) and αιμα (aima), the Greek for blood, and is found in more than sixty countries, carried by those of Italian, Greek, Southeast Asian, Indian, and Chinese descent, among others. Just under ten thousand people suffer from Cooley's anemia (the homozygous form of beta thalassemia, first described in 1925 by Dr. Thomas Cooley) in the United States, three hundred thousand worldwide. But close to two million people in the United States carry the genetic trait that can cause the disease in their children.

More than fifteen years ago, in the back of a Queens bakery a few families met from time to time to offer support for one another; their children suffered from thalassemia. Nowadays, through biweekly blood transfusions and the use of a drug called Desferal infused over a twelve-hour period out of every twenty-four hours to remove accumulated iron caused by the frequent transfusions, those with thalassemia live longer than in the past, though not without risk and difficulty.

But let us meet the protagonist of our story. In the fall of 1968, in the pediatric hematology clinic at Children's Hospital in Boston, David Nathan was confronted by the presence of a six-year-old boy, Dayem, who had achieved the height of a two-year-old. "His belly protruded between the buttons of his finely embroidered linen shirt, yet his elegant blue woolen shorts and matching jacket with brass buttons gave him the appearance of a doll-like English Public School boy. His legs looked like twigs, and on his tiny feet he wore baby shoes. As he moved carefully down the long corridor of the clinic, hand in hand with his mother, I could hear his noisy breathing ten feet away." It was the "ravishing smile" that "lit up his face" that David Nathan attended to, not the misshapen bones of his head and face that gave him the appearance of a gargoyle.

In Dayem's thalassemia, the hemoglobin genes fail to turn on. In response to the subsequent anemia, the bone marrow increases its effort to produce red blood cells. The head and face become distorted as the bones of the skull take up the task of red blood cell production. As the marrow cores of the bones expand, the bone is weakened and fractures occur. In the course of tracing out the trajectory of Dayem's life in relationship to his illness, we are presented with the contemporary history of medical research, with the role the federal government has played in the training of those who do basic medical and biological research, with the ways technology can change the nature of ethical debate, and with the immense contributions of places like the National Institutes of Health.

Yet it is through questions raised about hemoglobin whose answers "are enshrouded in the mists of evolution" that we have the most to learn. We still bear the rudiment of the single hemoglobin gene of our marine ancestors. Through a series of evolutionary changes starting approximately 450 million years ago, that single gene duplicated. And later, with more duplications and exquisite timing, certain of these genes commenced a dance of signals that holds true for us today: particular genes switch on during various foetal stages, and give way to others at birth. The persistence of such changes over millions of years accounts for our mammalian development.

Genes, Blood, and Courage: A Boy Called Immortal Sword ends as it should, through the adult voice of the patient with whom David Nathan has worked all these years and through the voice of Dayem's mother, both looking in retrospect over the years of coping with this complex illness.

For the reader who is not versed in the medical sciences, the strong narrative threads provide sufficient mapping to be of considerable interest. For those who wish to track the recent history of support for basic science and medical research in terms of current efforts to limit spending in these areas, there is much to be learned here. For those who wish to take the long view, to consider the remarkable journey of living

things during the long history of life on this planet, the study of tha-
lassemia and its survival in the population where it confers protection
against malaria is a fascinating tale.

Perhaps it will seem strange to some readers that a work so learned
and steeped in basic scientific knowledge should focus so strongly on the
human narrative in its closing chapters especially. But that, after all, is
or should be the true aim of medicine. "I'm often asked," Dr. Nathan
writes, "whether it is right to go to the ends of the technological earth
in an attempt to save or extend the life of one chronically ill child. The
same health dollars, it is argued, could be spent on vaccinations that
would prevent illness in thousands. . . . Yes, there are still huge inequities
in health care delivery and gross inadequacies in modern medicine's abil-
ity to heal. But if I could turn back the clock and start again, I would
walk through the same doors, and look down the same hallway, hop-
ing to catch another glimpse of a boy called Immortal Sword."

ROOT CAUSES

Stem Cells and the Tower

of Babel

*L*ike Babel, a "lunatic tower launched at the stars," the dream of finding the hematopoietic stem cell, progenitor of all other blood cells, has haunted researchers for years. To recover the source. As in language, to discover the single primal alphabet that lies behind our present discord, "behind the tumult of warring tongues which followed on the collapse of Nimrod's ziggurat."[9] To find the elusive primordial cell, rare in the bone marrow, that gives rise to platelet, neutrophil, macrophage, lymphocyte, erythrocyte. As from the mythology of languages, we imagine the hidden contours of the underlying speech of which our words are shards.

It is unity we are after: that a single cause might explain all of life; that we are descended from a common ancestor; that our language was once intelligible to all; that a unified field theory would show us a way to marry gravity with electromagnetism; that the formation of our planet could be traced back to a single knowable moment; that we would find at the bottom of the ocean a protoplasmic substance out of which complex life developed.

At times the evidence *has* pointed to beautiful underlying structures that organize immense bodies of information. Take the double helix, the molecular structure of the gene. That extraordinary double-hung staircase took Sir Thomas Browne's unwitting Chain of Being ("There is in this Universe a Stair, rising not disorderly or in confusion, but with a comely method and proportion."), a thoroughly eighteenth-century construct asserting the immutability of species, and brought it fully to life. Darwin's theory of evolution established the phylogenetic relationships among all forms of life, turning the key in the lock of Sir Browne's static proposition. The double helix, where a single chain serves as template for the synthesis of a complementary chain ("A structure this pretty just has to exist," wrote James Watson, one of its decipherers.), turned the key in that lock a second time.

Or take the recently discovered presence of a kind of genetic soup in the great oceans, virus particles. With the laying of the first Atlantic cable in the 1860s, a mistaken notion gained credence. It was thought that a living film on the sea bed consisted of an amorphous sheet of a protein compound, a diffused formless protoplasm. The notion in the nineteenth century that somehow the secret of the origin of life had been penetrated has given way in the twentieth to a more measured observation about a gene pool previously unnoticed.

QUESTIONS WITHOUT ANSWERS

Perhaps science is, after all, a history of questions. When looking for the origin of the blood, it is inevitable to ask about the embryonic development of blood and the persistence of those governing processes as a means of hemopoiesis into adult life. And it is logical to ask about the nature of a cell that can not only persist for the lifetime of the individual—or somehow pass along its function through some form of cell memory—but can also differentiate into the precursors of all blood cells. What determines the *way* the stem cell differentiates? A correlate of this asks: Is blood cell differentiation reversible? Can it go both ways—from stem cell to progenitor to specific blood cells back to progenitor and stem? Or is it a one-way street with an end product platelet or macrophage or lymphocyte? And these short-lived? And we would ask about the significance of locating the primordial cell: of what use would it be? And if there exists such a cell, why has it been so difficult to find?

SITES OF ORIGIN

In the mid-1800s it was thought that during fetal life the liver was the main blood-forming site. Later it was demonstrated that the first blood cells were formed in the extraembryonic tissues, the area opaca and the yolk sac. The attempt to look at embryonic processes rather than at cell lineages in the adult resulted in later controversy. By 1868, Neumann demonstrated that in the adult organism, the main site of blood cell formation was the bone marrow. As analytical techniques for recognizing the different cell types were not available until Paul Ehrlich applied the use of staining techniques, many questions went unanswered. Ehrlich introduced a dualistic concept—precursor marrow cells and precursor lymphatic cells. His was the first attempt to describe the ancestral cell, one that could maintain its own numbers by cell division and provide descendants that eventually mature into the various blood cells.

DIFFICULTY OF IDENTIFICATION AND PURIFICATION OF THE STEM CELL

The identification and purification of the stem cell proved to be especially elusive. To begin with, only a small proportion of cells in the bone marrow were thought to be stem cells. Second, there was uncertainty about markers associated with stem cells as distinct from more differentiated cells. Finally, there was a general inability to biologically assay for human stem cells.

WHY ATTEMPT TO ISOLATE THE HEMATOPOIETIC STEM CELL?

Potential uses resulting from the isolation of the stem cell include stem cell transplantation into the marrow of those with leukemia or cancer patients whose stem cells have been killed off by intensive chemotherapy. A spectacular advantage of the use of stem cells is the predicted absence of graft-versus-host disease. The stem cell, insufficiently differentiated, should not bring about an immune response. With regard to AIDS, stem cells may well restore the CD4 cells, the T-cells attacked by the AIDS virus, and return AIDS patients to far earlier stages of their disease, thus providing additional time should effective therapies become available for AIDS and extending life in any case. Moreover, stem cells could be engineered to contain normal copies of genes whose defects cause disease.

Research interests include attempting to identify growth factors associated with regeneration of the stem cell as well as growth factors associated with the early steps of dedication of the stem cell to a particular lineage.

TRACKING THE STEM CELL

L. L. Weissman, an immunologist at Stanford University, described the isolation of a human stem cell that can generate nearly every type of human blood cell when transplanted into the bone marrow of mice lacking an immune system. He used monoclonal antibodies as markers to identify the "cluster of identification" of each specific blood cell type. Various techniques were used to separate the cells by initially removing cells of dedicated lineage, i.e., differentiated cells. Once the differentiated cells were separated, the search was narrowed to a group of slow-growing cells, an indication that the cells' energy-producing mitochondria were merely idling, a trait characteristic of the long-lived stem cell.

When these human marrow cells were added to connective tissue cells taken from mouse marrow, it was found that one type of cell could give rise to all major blood-cell varieties. These cells were injected into the marrow of immunodeficient mice; others into human thymus tissue transplanted into a second group of immunodeficient mice. The first group of mice developed human white blood cells that normally arise form marrow, while the second group developed a normal collection of human T cells.

THE OUTLOOK FOR THE FUTURE

What remains to be tested is the success of these stem cells in producing a full complement of blood cells in human patients undergoing bone marrow transplants. Weissman has been given permission by one hospital to use the newly identified cells in clinical tests in the future. A particularly interesting use of this research has to do with hematotropic pathogens like HIV and HTLV-I where the stem cells could be genetically modified to introduce an antisense sequence or ribozyme that would prevent the proliferation of the pathogen in the stem cell or cells differentiated from the stem cells.

The patenting of both the stem cells and the isolation methods raises the possibility of serious legal challenge. Ethical and legal issues have become part of many scientific symposia these days and surely stem cell rights will be debated for some time to come.

After Babel and the loss of our ancient language, which "like a hidden spring seeks to force its way through the silted channels of our differing tongues," we make our way back through Darwin's tangled bank, clothed in multiple forms, to those progenitor cells capable not only of giving rise to all other cells in their particular repertoire but capable as well of ensuring their own long-term survival. And if, in our search for cause and origin and progenitor, we are confounded by complexity and proliferation and differentiation—the nature of life—we have only to remember Darwin's words at the close of *Origin of Species:* ". . . while this planet has gone circling on according to the fixed law of gravity, from so simple a beginning endless forms most beautiful and most wonderful have been and are being evolved."[10]

THE STATUE WITHIN

*S*igmund Freud wrote: "Every night human beings lay aside the wrappings in which they have enveloped their skin, as well as anything which they may use as a supplement to their bodily organs, for instance, their spectacles, their false hair and teeth. When they go to sleep they carry out an entirely analogous undressing of their minds and lay aside most of their psychical acquisitions. Thus on both counts they approach remarkably close to the situation in which they began life. The psychical state of a sleeping person is characterized by an almost complete withdrawal from the surrounding world and a cessation of all interest in it."[11]

François Jacob in his autobiography, *The Statue Within*, describes the reconstruction of his world each morning upon awakening: "Before I could perceive the world around me, see it, hear it, I had to reinvent it and set it in place, as much by imagination as by memory . . . To begin with, I reconstructed my room: it organized itself around my bed, a sort of impregnable citadel, a refuge from violence . . . The window had to be placed first . . . Before putting the ceiling on the box I had constructed, I might arrange the furniture in it." The parents' voices gave him the location of their room; horses' feet, the whereabouts of the street below. Beyond that, the greater world. And finally the recreation of the universe. Now, only now, could the child open his eyes. Such a strenuous labor faced him each morning. The obverse of Freud's account: how the self and its world is put back on once it is removed.

In the recollections and memories and early notions about the world of those who would later become scientists, one looks for clues. How are early curiosities and means of investigating the world manifested in the later work? How is that work *determined* by a particular orientation to the world established in childhood?

On a train traveling to Dijon to spend Christmas with grandparents, once again we encounter the child's need to reconstruct the world as though it does not exist with any permanence: "This whole landscape . . . was set up as the train approached and will be taken down once it has passed . . . besides the officially real, the everyday, the recognized, there existed another world that . . . duplicated this one but remained in the dark." Jacob describes it as a kind of "antechamber of the world."

At the age of fourteen, during religious services, he asks himself about the existence of God and considers a world devoid of a deity, "an empty heaven left an earth to fill." Once again he is required to construct the world. This notion is reinforced by his grandfather's words shortly before his death: "There's nothing. Nothing. The void. So my only hope is you."

School served to compartmentalize areas of knowledge, creating enormous barriers between history and mathematics, between the natural sciences and geography, offering closed systems. Once again, he set about constructing a synthesis, a coherent vision of what he was learning.

Having little sense of a vocation, Jacob completes a portion of medical training when the war begins. "Constructing a world around myself. Erecting piece by piece . . . first the milieu around me, the world of the everyday, with my room and house, city, the lycée, the university, their pasts and histories. Then understanding the country, the Republic with its institutions and its laws, it army and its justice. And suddenly the whole edifice has caved in." All that had seemed the basis of his existence crumbled in an instant. The deconstruction of the previous synthesis. He shipped out to England, joining the Free French and sailed for Senegal, serving as auxiliary medical officer. The year, 1940. Four years' service in North Africa and a long recovery in France following mortar wounds. Unable to walk, Jacob calls once more upon his old habit of constructing the world, taking long imaginary walks across Paris.

"Proceed down to the Seine. Walk as far as the Louvre . . ." He stops before the door to his family home. He had no news of his father or other family members in several years. At the age of twenty-six years, Jacob had no earnings and no profession.

In an effort to obtain a post, having decided on biological research, Jacob is offered a research fellowship at the Pasteur Institute and at the age of thirty begins the introductory survey course, the "Great Course," in bacteriology, virology, and immunology. After several failed attempts, he succeeds in winning a place at the Pasteur with Andre Lwoff who is then working on the induction of the prophage, a vocabulary that is entirely mysterious to Jacob.

At this point in *The Statue Within* the work becomes a record of scientific work, a tracing of experimental work and mentors leading up to Jacob's major contribution, an understanding of genetic regulatory mechanisms in the synthesis of proteins. Along the way we encounter Jacques Monod, Max Delbruck—"Pope" of the "Phage Church—" Salvador Luria, James Watson, Francis Crick, and others in the forefront of DNA research. Here physicists worked with biochemists, discipline lines were crossed and crossed again, with the insights from each augmenting the work of all. Here too Jacob learns about the difference between American science and European. "No constraints, no ceremonies. No hollow speeches, no weighty terms . . . scientific aspect . . . compact and vigorous. With what was unimaginable in Europe: young students who did not hesitate to challenge the official stars . . . All these boys and girls were ravenous and elbowing their way along. A sort of horde unleashed on science like a pack of greyhounds after a cardboard rabbit." About the double helix he says: "The structure was of such simplicity, such perfection, such harmony, such beauty even, and biological advantages flowed from it with such rigor and clarity, that one could not believe it untrue."

To the question of why one would expend one's life energy in science, Jacob speaks of the attempt to understand a world that is veiled. It is a response to a "metaphysical need for coherence and unity in a universe one seeks to possess but does not even manage to grasp." And harking back to his habit of childhood Jacob tells us that "science meant for me . . . tirelessly rebuilding the world while taking account of reality."

> Contrary to what I had long believed, the process of experimental science does not consist in explaining the unknown by the known, as in certain mathematical proofs. It aims, on the

contrary, to give an account of what is observed by the prop-
erties of what is imagined. To explain the visible by the invis-
ible. And it is through the evolution of the invisible, through
an appeal to new hidden structures, with hypothetical prop-
erties, that science proceeds. Lightning, for example, was
long considered an expression of the wrath of Zeus before it
was viewed as resulting from differences in electrical poten-
tial between the sky and the earth. Infectious diseases were
thought to be the effect of evil spells cast over sick people
before the role of microbes and viruses was invoked. It was,
thus, the properties of these hidden structures, of these invis-
ible forces, on which the imagination could play by con-
structing its theories.[12]

Thus the child who had constructed each morning the universe around
himself before he permitted his eyes to open, the scientist who had been
involved for the first time in the history of biology in establishing a chro-
mosomal map by three independent methods, comes around in the end
to an understanding that was with him from the beginning. "The world
of science, like that of art or religion, was a world created by the human
imagination, but within very strict constraints imposed both by nature
and by the human brain. As if this science endeavored not to photograph
nature, but to paint it. To decompose it in order to refashion it by every
means at its disposal."

A Place Called Gehinom

Writing the Holocaust

auch ohne/Sprache

1

*N*orma Rosen, in her collected essays, *Accidents of Influence,* writes in "Notes Toward a Holocaust Fiction": "Whether or not we're crazy with the weight and grief of it . . . we are astonishingly sane. Only sanity remembers. Sanity makes a home for the dead." And in her essay "The Second Life of Holocaust Imagery," she writes:

One day, perhaps a young woman nursing her baby in her own safe house, who has read Cynthia Ozick's "The Shawl," will feel the pain of that mother's sight of her starved infant in a way that is immediate and profound . . . though she and her child are protected and healthy in America, she will infuse her own experience with the terror these stories convey, a second life of art. And since that art is a Holocaust re-creation, the woman's response will be a Holocaust memory of a sort, and we must let it be. And then perhaps a novelist will write of that woman's experience. And so connectedness and continuity evolve. The manner of it may disturb us with its

impurity, but in the end this may be the deepest kind of on-
going Holocaust memorial that we can have.[1]

How *are* we to make a home for our dead, to abide their living mem-
ory? How to appropriate what we have not directly experienced, yet has
shaped our lives? The home for my dead began to take form one day
when I was seven. In 1941. It was then I found my parents sitting in
stunned silence on the wooden stairs between the first and second floors
of our house one afternoon. I had no idea why my father was home in
the middle of the day, nor what event or knowledge had brought them
together that way. I gradually began to realize—as children do no mat-
ter how well secrets are kept—that our large family in Lithuania, those
who had not come to the United States earlier, would not come. Ever.
I remember discussions in Yiddish in my grandmother's house, men
standing up, heated debates, desperation. I know efforts of rescue were
underway. I wondered why English schoolchildren came to live with
American families, went to my school, when Jewish children from my
family in Lithuania never came. Around that time I began to imagine the
girl, my counterpart, my Lithuanian sister, who I might very well have
been. And I have carried that sister with me all my life.

2

Not until now—fifty-six years later—is there direct corroboration that
the impression of a seven-year-old child bore the truth. On this very day,
a cousin hands me a letter that his father received. It was sent from
Kovno (Kaunas), Lithuania on December 28, 1940. It was the last let-
ter ever to be received from my cousin's uncle, Jacob Wolpe. Of his entire
family, only one person would survive, his daughter.

     Under the Molotov-Ribbentrop Pact, the Soviet-Nazi treaty of 1939,
Eastern Europe was partitioned. The Baltic states came under the juris-
diction of the Soviets. The Soviet occupation began on June 15, 1940.
A year later, June 22, 1941, Nazi Germany attacked the Soviet Union.
"Operation Barbarossa" opened its assault on Lithuania. The Red Army
fled. In the following days, with the arrival of German occupation
forces, the entire Jewish populations of over 150 villages and towns were
massacred. In a document, "Total List of the Executions Carried Out in
the Area of Einsatzkommando 3 by 1 December 1941,"[2] we find exe-
cution lists by date, town, men, women, and children—and a summary:

"Jews liquidated—exclusively by partisans—through pogroms and exe-
cutions before the take-over of Security Police tasks by Einsatzkom-
mando 3: 4,000; Total [executions]: 137,346." We read: "4 October
1941: Kauen—Fort IX [Kaunas/Kovno]: 315 Jews, 712 Jewesses, 818
Jewish children (Punitive operation because a German policeman was
shot at in the ghetto); 29 October 1941: Kauen—Fort IX: 2,007 Jews,
2,920 Jewesses, 4,273 Jewish children (cleansing the ghetto of super-
fluous Jews)." The list is long and detailed.

Eight months following the sending of the letter, Jacob Wolpe and
his family would be forced to move into the Kovno Ghetto; from there
to Dachau and Stutthof Concentration Camps. Father and son would
die in Dachau. Mother would die in Stutthof. The two daughters,
following a forced march, would be put on a ship in the Baltic Sea where
they would be deprived of food and water for eight days and then
thrown overboard. One would swim to shore, a tiny burlap sack at-
tached to the wrist of her right arm. Inside, two broken combs —all that
remained of her mother and sister, some thread, a lipstick case, a piece
of soap. She would be found by a British solder as she lay with her body
partly covered by water, her sister drowning moments before reaching
the shore in Kiel, Germany. The soldier, thinking the girl to be dead,
kicked her: "This one moves." She is taken to a hospital.

Later, in Italy, after the war, a U.S. Army captain interviewed her.
"Have you no family?" he asked. "No place where you can go?" She
answered that she had no one. But then she remembered an uncle in the
United States, her father's brother whom she had once met. Perhaps an
uncle, she responded. The soldier offered to try to contact the uncle in
America. The girl thought nothing would come of it, that the young man
would forget or be unable to help. But when he returned to the United
States, he put a notice in a New York newspaper and by the best of
fortunes the uncle learned of the existence of his niece. He wired the girl:
"Please come to America. Be well. Have courage. We love you." The
next day her uncle sent another wire: "Please advise me your need. Will
do everything possible to help. With love." But it was not until four
years after liberation that she received a visa to enter the United States.

The letter sent from her father to his brother in Washington, D.C.,
in 1940 begins this way: "In our days, to receive a letter from relatives
is a source of great joy . . . a cause for celebration. It gives us the feel-
ing that we are not so lonely in this world. You mentioned in your
letter the Garden of Eden but you forget that there is also such a place
called hell—Gehinom. . . . It is very urgent for us to see you . . . Please,

we beg of you again to do everything in your power to make it possible for us to meet with you … now it can still be done. … Good wishes from our mother, she sends you her cordial blessings. Your brother, Jacob Wolpe."

It is chilling to read this letter now, with its coded language that it might get past the censors. To know that the family here knew the situation and could do little. To recognize that those in Lithuania were fully aware of what lay in store for them. To feel the sluice gate close. The opportunity for rescue beyond possibility.

3

It never seemed appropriate to try to represent or engage directly with the Holocaust in my writing; yet it was always there. It colored all I did. When I nursed my child, I thought about how Jewish women in the Holocaust were not permitted to have children, how those who became pregnant risked the child's death by starvation or worse. When I buried my father I said a grateful prayer that he died here, died of natural causes, died at the end of a long and useful life. I was grateful he did not die in the Holocaust.

When I made love I thought of stories my survivor friend told me—how before the transport to Auschwitz left, an older girl made love with each of the young boys so they would not go to their deaths uninitiated. I thought about the day he took my hand as we walked down the hall at the university, a beautiful April day, "like when I was in the camps," he told me, "I am so happy." How could that be? I asked him. He told me that when he was in Theresienstadt, a place where he had traded his ration of bread for a copy of Shakespeare, he had entered puberty. And he climbed up on a wall that was guarded by soldiers with machine guns, he took off his clothes and lay in the sun and relished his happiness.

4

How can we write about the Holocaust? Adorno speaks of the "barbarism" in "the so-called artistic representation" of the Shoah. Such representation "contains the power … to extract pleasure out of it. … Through aesthetic principles of stylization … the unimaginable ordeal appears as if it had some meaning; it is transfigured and stripped of some of its horror and this in itself already does an injustice to the victims."[3]

The poet Robert Pinsky has spoken about the pressure, if not to say something new, to justify the purpose of speaking about the Holocaust. Poetry, he tells us, contains stories, narratives, but it is quite distinct from linear storytelling. "In poetry the stories tend to come in contracted or conflicting gobbets. They collide with one another. They are interrupted at odd moments . . . change direction quickly." Can Adorno's dictum be countermanded by that quality of poetry to "interrupt the story, to change the subject? To transform the subjective." The characteristic action of lyric poetry is not to "amplify but to transform. [It is to this very notion of transformation that Adorno raises his objections] And to provide a sense of how material endlessly can raise new questions, avoiding facile resolution. Poetry through its capacity to change direction quickly always provides a reminder that there is another question to be asked, still another way to view what has happened." Poetry, Pinsky tells us, teaches us how to ask appropriate questions in memorable ways.[4]

5

Forget about the past, we are told. How can you make any progress if you are always tied to the past? we are asked. Can we be released from the past by our intentional and selective "forgetting"? And is remembering any kind of guarantee against future genocide?

FORGETTING

How sweet is the landscape
of forgetting: no
trembling arrow
soaring from the past—
the present
forming beneath our fingertips.

Let the past be severed
like the head
of a chicken, only the dumb

clucking of that head going off
in the barnyard like a fizzled
canister
and the clumsy body propped
on its scaly legs,
improbable corpus scattering
to the four winds.

Let all judgment be
made of the bones
of the moment.

Witness us like the man
who steps off into the future.
Or pity us carping at his side
like those who stood on either
side of the saviour
the shadow of the past strangled
in the trees.

6

In Lithuania, I learned that memory resides in the physical place. That
I could not be whole until I had put my feet down on the earth where
they had lived. Until I had knelt in the cemetery. Taken the broad leaves
growing there, cleared the moss and earth off the gravestones until I
could see their faces, the holy words, the names in Hebrew. Until I had
walked in their streets, touched the places of massacre, gathered the
earth in my hands.

Yet in these acts comes the terrible knowledge. That a landscape
so fraught with human suffering could go on. That the sun would not
have burned itself out, in the face of such slaughter would not have
shunned our earth. That life itself could continue. That the whole
world would not be so contaminated by what had taken place that it
would be extinguished.

Paul Danaceau, sent to Israel in 1961 to cover the Eichmann trial, has said it more eloquently than anyone I know.

> This is the land of survivors.
> And that there is a sun, that there is grass, that there are trees and flowers, hills and homes; but mostly, that there are children, seems a terrifying and grotesque joke; as if all were placed here upon barren land and under empty heavens as a lure for the final destruction of the people; the ultimate abandonment. For the hills of the survivors are the hills of bodies without heads and heads without bodies; and the sun, the cold and pagan sun that the black chimney touches daily with its offering of human incense; and the grass and flowers the hallucinations of a tortured madmen; and the homes the freezing barracks that compress the screaming, the moaning, the despairing and the dead so that, once and for all, suffering shall know its own futile limits; and the children, an innocence that never was. So that now, whatever is, whatever lives, seems a profanity and mere presence a violation of the memory, as if only by *not* being could the land—and the people—keep faith. And such was the past, so misplaced and misshapen the guilt, that the innocent see in their own pitiful survival the greatest sin of all. "Why me? Why did I live? What sin did I commit?" Only the desert speaks with an honesty, the honesty of barrenness and a ravaged despair. Where there are only rocks and an occasional light-green tree: a fragile freak in a white-yellow desolation. Where there are no sounds and few motions: only the black vultures swooping in silence, the Dead Sea rippling in silence. Where the heat rises into the eyes and back into the brain until it is seen; and the heat blinds. "Breathe deeply, my lambs,"—the instructions to the children in the gas chamber—and again the heat stabs at the lungs, presses on all sides like an unbearable round vise, and you are unable to move. Then you wait against sheets of twisted rock that rise high along the cliffs: dry, massive crusts of bleached earth, as if even the earth itself had been slashed open and drained.[5]

7

What right to appropriate the Holocaust? I have asked all my life. Let
the dead tell their story. Let the survivors tell their stories; I mustn't. And
how can we make poetry of it? Isn't that worse than silence? And if
we write, in what language can it be said? Paul Celan created a new lan-
guage for his poetry—hermetic, sealed from within, atom flares rising
from within the cell of language and being swallowed again. Nelly
Sachs brought the German of her poems into the vicinity of the liturgi-
cal, the cabalistic, until in memory they seem to wear the clothing
of Hebrew.

Now I want to ask different questions. How the Lithuanian looked
and what words he spoke when to his dismay after the massacre of the
Jews of Keidan he bought three bags for little money and discovered they
contained tfillin. He had no idea what tfillin were and rode up over the
bridge in Keidan and threw them into the Obelis river. I want to know
exactly how the neighbors came into the houses of Jews when they had
been taken away and killed, how they decided what they would take,
what a mother said to her child or a husband to his wife about what they
were doing. And afterward, years afterward, what they told themselves
and their children about what had taken place.

And those who survived—what is the nature of their remembering?
Charlotte Delbo, in *La Memoire et les Jours,* speaks of past events not
relegated to the distance but always next to her: "Auschwitz is there,
unalterable, precise . . . enveloped in the skin of memory, an imperme-
able skin that isolates it from my present self. Unlike the snake's skin,
the skin of memory does not renew itself. Oh, it may harden further . . .
Alas, I often fear lest it grow thin, crack, and the camp get hold of me
again . . . I live within a twofold being."[6] When the skin of memory fails
to hold, she becomes the person she was in the death camp—frozen,
hungry, filthy, exhausted. In dreams, the act of will cannot hold, the life
alongside her life breaks through. Yet in the dream she cries out and the
sound of her cry wakes her. She emerges from Auschwitz once again.
And gives voice to her experience *in extremis.*

And what is the nature of the survivor's loss? Jean Amery, who was
tortured by the SS, speaks of the loss of "trust in the world," in *At the
Mind's Limits.* By social contract the other person will "respect my
physical . . . my metaphysical being. The boundaries of my body are
also the boundaries of my self. My skin surface shields me against the
external world. If I am to have trust, I must feel on it only what I *want*

to feel." He points out that in most situations in life, when we are injured, there is the expectation of help. Yet with the "first blow from a policeman's fist, against which there can be no defense and which no helping hand will ward off, a part of our life ends and it can never again be revived." Torture, he tells us, is the inversion of the social world. "A slight pressure by the tool-wielding hand is enough to turn the other—along with his head, in which are perhaps stored Kant and Hegel, and all nine symphonies, and the World as Will and Representation—into a shrilly squealing piglet at slaughter. When it has happened and the torturer has expanded into the body of his fellow man and extinguished what was his spirit, he himself can then smoke a cigarette or sit down to breakfast or, if he has the desire, have a look in at the World as Will and Representation." What is lost, Amery tells us, is trust in the world. One cannot be at home here. "That one's fellow man was experienced as the antiman remains in the tortured person as accumulated horror. It blocks the view into a world in which the principle of hope rules."[7]

Peter Kenez, in *Varieties of Fear,* a memoir about growing up in Hungary under Nazism and Communism, when asked what he feared responded that he was only afraid of other human beings. Erik Erikson spoke of his hope for a public conviction that the "mutilation of a child's spirit" and the way this "undercuts the life principle of trust" will be considered the "most deadly of all possible sins."

8

Why go back to the past? I am asked. Why not let it go? After seven hundred years—as a result of an earthquake—the Cimabue frescoes lining the vault of the basilica of St. Francis, works that heralded the Renaissance and stood as monuments for all the world, lie in crumbled ruin on the dry earth of Assisi as if to say, Don't count on us. We search for meaning among those colored fragments.

Susan Sontag wrote in "Unguided Tour": "Devotion to the past is one of the more disastrous forms of unrequited love." Unrequited? I am walking into the town of wooden houses where once my family lived. I have stopped before a small wooden house, painted yellow. I take off my shoes and enter the kitchen where freshly churned butter sits on the counter and opposite, a pan of water drawn from the well and covered with a delicate cloth. I think of my grandmother's house on the Sabbath, the yeast dough rising in an enamel pan on the radiator in the kitchen. These two kitchens, like two sheets of paper, like two photographs, one domain mapped onto another. Ola, in childhood, visited the houses of my family. She remembers them—the birthmark on the right side of Shimon's face, Leah his sister (my mother's first cousin), the celebration of holidays, the Jews gathered up and slaughtered. "The priest told us not to worry our hearts, that it was the fate of the Jews for the suffering of Christ. But I did not believe it." She is the key to my past. I gather her words, they are the colored shards on the floor of Assisi, they are the remnants, they are all I can know. But they are enough. They are proof that I am real. That I have lived in the world. That I have come from somewhere. From someone.

9

Yet when the past is a graveyard, a remnant, what can be found there? What is to be learned there? Though most of those who were killed had no resting place, apart from the massacre pits where they were thrown and unburied and burned, still it seemed possible to find the cemeteries, to read the gravestones. Even these were destroyed, used for foundations of houses, for walls and staircases. In a town in Lithuania, an American whose father came from that place hired a local man to care for the cemetery. "Your employee, an alcoholic, has brought junk to the cemetery, over fifty cinder blocks, and set them up as gravestones," a woman wrote to him. The "guardian" hired to clean the cemetery had, in his own way, created an act of restoration. For the depleted resting places, the long-buried separated from their names and the names of their fathers, this man had reconstructed the world aboveground. So, even in this essentially unconscious act, in an act so complex as to be almost impossible to interpret, is it from regret or a sense of responsibility that the drunk tries to make amends, that without bodies or caskets or burial shrouds he sets up scrap cement to take the place of the destroyed and sacred burial stones? Or is it a matter of deepest irony that centuries of religious life and observance in Lithuania have come to this—an empty, meaningless scrap of sand and water, without inscription, without rootedness, floats atop the earth of the former cemetery? Or even worse, a kind of golem cemetery, these misshapen structures a hideous perversion?

10

Once I was asked to testify in a medical malpractice case. The patient had gone in for elective surgery, minor surgery, and during the operation had stopped breathing. Despite a series of warning signals that are in general use during such procedures—whether because these warnings were ignored or because the warning systems failed—the patient stopped breathing for a sufficiently long time that she suffered serious brain damage and never regained consciousness. During the course of the trial it became clear that we would never know exactly what had transpired. We would have versions of the events—the role of the anaesthesiologist, the placing of the endotracheal tube, the monitoring system, the role of the surgeon, nurses, technicians, the view of the hospital administrator, the family, acquaintances, statistics with regard to risks for this particular type of surgery, track records of anaesthesiologist and surgeon. And from these versions, the jury was asked to assess not precisely what had happened, but whether the patient was entitled to damages.

I often think of that case when I consider events in Lithuania during the Second World War, particularly those events that took place during the several days between the departure of the Russians after a year's occupation and the arrival of the Germans in June 1941. We may know very well the massacre places in every town where Jews lived. We can find the bones of the Jews in those towns. We do not need forensic scientists to do studies. And there are still enough of those living witnesses to learn what happened. But we are left with versions of the truth. Haven't I been told by well-meaning Lithuanians in towns that were once Jewish shtetls of my family that Jews were killed because they had been responsible for the exile to Siberia of so many Lithuanians. Yet we know that the proportion of Jews exiled to Siberia was far greater than that of Lithuanians. Yes, it is true that the NKVD (Soviet secret police) had Jewish participants; Stalin was clever.

11

Walter Benjamin has written: "Truth is not a process of exposure that destroys the secret, but a revelation which does justice to it. The content of truth does not emerge in an unveiling . . ."

Who is telling the truth? An elderly man from Vandzhigola? I am sit-
ting on a low stool near his tiled oven plucking dried beans from their
ghostly pods. It is a cold November day. "They killed the Jews. And then
they were coming with their carts and wagons and horses and they were
taking their property. They were taking everything, but where the things
are now, nobody knows. After they were killed, the property was sold.
It was taken to a shop."

"When it comes to the dangerous times, the richest families [Jew-
ish] were bringing to the Lithuanians and Poles the most valuable things.
My wife didn't accept anything. Because we were not sure what would
happen. And people took, people took. All the killings were performed
by the local people. From the villages. And then they were selling the
bloody clothes. Everything was for sale. But the people didn't buy the
bloody clothes. They were taking out the teeth, the golden teeth."

"How did they remove them?"

"I didn't see. But it was said."

"And after the killing?"

"They didn't do anything to Poles and the people who were doing
the killing. They came back to live their lives. Or some escaped together
with the Germans. Germans were smart. They gave them guns. And took
pictures."

This is the same town about which my mother's youngest sister—
the only surviving sibling of that family—tells a little story. When she
was a child in America and would plead with her Lithuanian parents for
ice cream money, they would smile at one another and say to the child:
"Go and ask them in Vandzhigola! Pack your suitcase and go to
Vandzhigola!" She had always assumed that they had invented this
town. But when I looked on the map, I discovered there was such a
place; it had been ninety-five percent Jewish. So I went to visit
Vandzhigola. "Here is the rabbi's house," a woman tells us. "And this
was a dairy farm owned by a Jew, here across the road. And here, the
shochet lived." Somehow I had disappointed my aunt; I had taken away
the imaginary town that her parents had invented. I had made it a real
place. Perhaps that is what is happening to me as well—the myth of
place, the myth of origin is becoming real.

Michael Steinlauf writes in "Beyond the Evil Empire: Freedom to
Remember or Freedom to Forget?":

> First and foremost, there is the powerful, pervasive sense of
> place. Cities, towns, streets, marketplaces, courtyards, mez-

uzahs still outlined over doorways; synagogues and cemeteries . . . the Vistula River, cutting through the Polish heartland, whose waters, the writer Sholem Asch once declared, spoke to him in Yiddish; these and countless other sites saturated with the visible and invisible traces of Jewish presence, are all still there, a Jewish geography as yet unmapped, but as real as any. Side-by-side, sometimes in the same places, are the death sites: remnants of camps, graves, crematoria. Can we deal with this? Can we finally accept the challenge of seeing everything, the life as well as the death?[8]

12

One survivor told me: "I remember practicing to remain still so I could be carried out of the Kovno Ghetto in a potato sack on my mother's back when she went out in the morning to forced labor." Her rescue took place shortly after the Children's Action in March 1944 when the majority of children who had survived until that time were killed. Some children were given injections to sedate them as they were transported in tool sacks to safety. Though only six percent of Jews in Lithuania survived, the survival of a single child depended upon the cooperation of not only the family who took in the child, but of dozens of others, the silence of a whole village. In some cases twenty or more people were involved in the rescue of one child. Often a child could not be kept in any one place for more than a night or two.

Another, Yocheved Inciuriene, has written:

> To survive the German occupation in Kaunas and in the villages, I was helped without doubt by my knowledge of Lithuanian, my youthful daring bordering almost on recklessness: If everything is forbidden for me, then I do as I like. I knew and read all the German police orders but in my soul I could not agree that it is forbidden for me to live but not my friend Jamina. To resist all forbiddings, to run and hide forced me not to fear for my life, but my inner conviction that I have to survive. All whom I mention hid me, fed me and cared for me, risking their and their families' lives. Some did this out of elementary humanity, friendship or pity—others out of their political conviction that the Jewish genocide is the shame of the twentieth century. Fate brought me together in those terrible days with very good people, some Lithuanians, some Poles.[9]

Which is the truth? Is it something we can open in our hands, a thing to be peeled back, layer by layer until it finally reveals itself. "The true measure of life is memory," Walter Benjamin tells us. "Looking backwards, it runs through life like lightning." But who, I ask, can remember what has happened here?

13

I have climbed down into a pit in the Ponar Forest where one hundred thousand people—most of them Jews—have been murdered. I am kneeling in the excavated, exposed earth. I have come alone to this place. I gather up a handful of earth and when I open my hand I discover a nub of bone. This is the place where those Jews who were forced to dig up the bodies of those who had been killed and arrange them on pyres and burn them to destroy the evidence of what was done here—this is where they had lived and where, when they attempted to tunnel out, they were killed by mines placed within the tunnel.

As I knelt there, I became aware that I was not alone. I turned and looked up to the rim of the pit where a family was standing, looking at me as though I were a ghost. I was startled by their presence. I spoke to them in Lithuanian, but they did not reply, and slowly I climbed up out of the pit. When I reached the place where they were standing, I turned and walked out of the forest where so many had died. They watched me silently until I was out of sight. I felt as though I had come back from the dead. That they were right. I was one of the lost souls too.

14

Chaim Grade returned to the Vilna Ghetto after its destruction. "The seven narrow little streets hung on me like seven stone chains." What does he hope to find here? What will this place say to him? "I go home, and gliding behind me comes the ghetto, with all its broken windows, like blind people groping their way along the walls." He has the sense he has left something behind in the ghetto and returns, notices something rustling at his feet. "Crumpled leaves from Hebrew prayerbooks, scattered pages from sacred tomes." Two years since the ghetto was destroyed. ". . . the pages are still wandering around. It seems to me as if the dead came back at night to study their books and scrolls." He senses that those who have died have torn out the pages and given them to the wind, that they might fall to his hands, that he should see what has become of the People of the Book. "Perhaps the tears that drenched the Techinas will live again for me, perhaps my own boyhood face will shine out . . . and I will be able to go on dreaming over a book of wonder tales."[10]

15

It has been written that "when the past is seriously contended among different groups of stakeholders in a society or when the past has the potential of assigning guilt to large groups of people, public history becomes contentious. Its stigma may be dispelled through outright denial, comparisons with similar horrors that thereby render them relatively harmless, by creating boundaries through a distancing from the events in time, place or persons or even by wearing the stigma as a badge of honor."[11]

It is no accident that memorials to those who died have been defiled, defaced, or stolen. The long silence under communism cannot be maintained much longer. Even in the few years of independence, there are deep changes in the society, groundswells.

Simon Schama wrote in *Landscape and Memory:* "Historians are supposed to reach the past through texts . . . through things that are safely caught in the bell jar of academic convention. Look: don't touch. But one of my best-loved teachers . . . had always insisted on directly experiencing 'a sense of place,' of using 'the archive of the feet'."[12]

For me, there is no replacement for that. The miracle is that it is possible to walk in Lithuania in my lifetime. I shall always be grateful for that, no matter what there is still to face in that country.

That children with no context for their memories, no language, not even the sense of what it meant to have a mother, or father, that such children, nurtured in the landscape of brutality and death could grow into adulthood, could be sane; that a little girl who lived in the forests of Poland for two years, sometimes in a hole in the ground, a child who risked certain death in order to hear the sound of human voices from time to time, could cross over into adulthood intact—there are no words for saying what it is about the human spirit that it can make this passage.

As for writing the Holocaust, perhaps Paul Celan understood it best—"*auch ohne/Sprache*"—even without language must it be written. It must be kept, imprinted in the language of memory. But memory itself is not the guardian who will keep us from devising the harm we bring to one another.

HOLOCAUST

Could we register birds
migrating,
could we count them all,
or ants in the ant hill,
or bees returning to the hive,
or the dead rocking in the earth.

ON MURANOWSKA STREET

I have always loved particulars: the angels
bearing a martyr's palm, the way the hair
of the worshipers forms waves or
filaments, the flowers embroidered
on your sleeve. Even my sleep
contains them: the pointed teeth
of mice, a black camera aimed
at my grief. Yet when you ask for the truth
I summon words empty
as air as if I were guarding a sorrow,
encapsulating it that nothing
might come into its vicinity, letting it
ripen. Like the foot of this woman swollen
with callouses, bearing
bits of earth and tar, thorns, remnants
salvaged in it like the map
of the world, pebbles filled with carbon
when the earth was young, fern still

coiled in sandstone. Never mind that he draws
this foot to his lips and kisses the world
that lies embedded in it, or that beneath
the bellies rolling down to her knees
he sees only the loveliest bones hidden
there, caverns and wetlands he traverses
easily, moving from opening
to opening like a bird metabolizing at a rate
too high to measure. He does not hear
the rifle fire behind her nor the fleeting
sound of hooves. He does not see
twenty men standing on Muranowska
Street, their hands raised in the air.

Then
for Paul Celan

I think just because you are
coming I can write the poem
of the creation of the world I
can put the Seine in my river poem
the temple of the cobblestone
cobblestones of liberation
in my poem because you are
coming. I think I can put the prefect
of police in my poem harvest
of exile golden badges sutured
like leaves into the bodies
of children. But it is not
like a door opening this poem not
willing like a finger dipped
in the earth. River this Seine
why do the threadbare badges cover
the surface of water
like petals river who touches
every groping heart are you the one

who received the poet his armful
of crystals that night in April
before the last darkness
of winter was washed off river
the poet walked that night
letting off breathing opening
his death like a jar.

1941

You decide to crawl out
from the haystack
where you are hiding.

To come up for air. Even
the lowliest fish
of the sea is allowed to pull

the residue of air
into its blood. For some
it is too late—the pitchfork

of the farmer pushed in and
in. But you scramble
to the top of a chimney

pot where two storks
have made their immense
nest. You can be seen in the flat

landscape. You take no trouble
to conceal yourself.
This is before the farmer

raises his rifle, before your
expulsion from this world
into the next. You warm yourself

among the storks. Prophet
among birds, your world ajar,
you read the sun trying

to go down, the moon
with its hem caught
on the horizon. For

a moment, in perfect stasis,
high on your absurd perch
you are still breathing.

THE ROOTS OF RESISTANCE

Le Chambon

*W*hat is missing at Le Chambon are the Jews. One sees the place well enough, the steep streets of a village and the police who have come to arrest Pastor Trocme seated at the dinner table because the pastor's wife insisted that the evening meal be taken. One sees the townspeople coming to bring gifts to him, in defiance of the Vichy regime, unveiling once again the human, insisting on it. One sees the large wooden door through which the strangers arrived, the seal to the left of the door, and the small inner opening to the presbytery. But one never sees them, their faces. The presence of these shadows accumulates in the pages of Philip Halle's book *Lest Innocent Blood Be Shed*— the sounds of their whispers, their Babel of languages.

In Le Chambon during the Second World War, the Jews were joined to each family like a second soul. They passed through the houses of strangers. If some survived the Nazis, it was due to a pastor, to a town of people. In each house a Jew stopped on his way to somewhere else, on his way from somewhere. He did not stand still and declare: This is my home. For if he did, he risked his own survival. And in those times there was no homeland, no place for him to go.

When the decision was made in Le Chambon, a small town in southern France, to place the town and its inhabitants in grave jeopardy and eventually to save some twenty-five hundred Jewish men, women, and children, the Chambonnais had been rehearsing the decision for centuries. The townspeople of Le Chambon were an anomaly in France as descendants of the Huguenots who had been persecuted since the sixteenth century. Each person had fought his own battle against those who would crush him. Their rebellion was whole. It was not a a matter of a leader establishing the position of resistance for the rest, but a position that rested squarely within each inhabitant of the town.

One example of just how reliable was this individual consciousness may be seen in the transformation of Bible study leaders. There were thirteen groups led by youngsters for the purpose of study. When the Germans conquered France, these groups became the communications network and their leaders, the moving spirits of the rescue operation. During the occupation, Trocme gave most of his instruction (Bible and resistance!) to these leaders.

Pastor Trocme saw to it that he was the only person in Le Chambon who knew of the entire operation, that the groups operated independently of one another, so that if one leader was caught and tortured, he would not reveal enough to destroy the whole rescue machine. Each leader had to make swift, intelligent decisions on his own when Trocme was not available.

There are two important lessons to be learned from the Chambonnais. The first, that one must be prepared to be human. The second, that in the act of resistance, timing is the crucial factor.

I have heard it said by concentration camp survivors that one must be wary of the first, smallest injustice. Through the entryway of the first injustice does the next come. And the next. The decision to act in the face of injustice does not come when a man is being shoved into a ravine with a bullet in his neck. To act against injustice—to express one's humanity—must begin early. And it must be learned. It has been said that it is the work of a whole lifetime to become human.

Pastor Trocme tells a story: In 1921, he was in the French army on a mapping mission in Morocco. He was surprised to be issued a gun and cartridges, and in the name of nonviolence left his equipment at the depository. In the desert, when asked where his weapons were, he announced that as a Christian he could not kill. He was told by his lieutenant that he had endangered the lives of the entire group by his action. He was already committed to this military campaign. He should have made such a decision earlier.

This conversation in the desert was a turning point in Trocme's thinking. It taught him that the ethical commandment against killing had to be obeyed as early as possible if it was to be obeyed effectively. It taught him that nonviolence could in fact increase violence if it was not chosen in the right way at the right time.

The first refusals were small. The town refused to ring the bell of the church to show gratitude to Marshal Philippe Petain, the head of the Vichy state. The people refused to salute the flag with the stiff-armed, palm-down salute of the Fascists. Thus was the intimate, unglamorous "kitchen struggle" of Le Chambon begun. For those who had suffered the Saint Bartholomew's Day Massacre of 1572, for those who had for three centuries been stripped of their property, liberty, and lives, who were persecuted, arrested, hanged, or burned, often in the town of Le Chambon itself, these acts of resistance were cherished.

When the Vichy police came to take Pastor Trocme to prison, the people of Le Chambon came one by one to bring him gifts: precious packets of candles, chocolate biscuits, sardines, stockings, a roll of toilet paper. During the first evening in the camp he discovered that verses of consolation from the Bible had been written on the toilet paper. These verses reminded him that he was still part of Le Chambon, that he was still human.

Elie Wiesel tells the story of a group of Jews who had gathered to pray in a synagogue in Nazi-occupied Europe. "As the service went on, suddenly a pious Jew who was slightly mad—for all pious Jews were by then slightly mad—burst in through the door. Silently he listened for a moment as the prayers ascended. Slowly he said: 'Shh, Jews! Do not pray so loud! God will hear you. Then He will know that there are still some Jews left alive in Europe.'"

Emil Fackenheim tells that "secular Jewish existence after Auschwitz is threatened with a madness no less extreme than that which produces a prayer addressed to God, yet spoken softly lest it be heard." It is strange to look to such a town, to the Chambonnais, as a place and a people whose humanity and caring were as natural and at home as the impatient words of Magda Trocme, the pastor's wife, who said to the first Jew who came to her door for help: "Naturally, come in and come in."[13]

Instructions for the Messiah

CROSSING OVER

When my first child tore
loose from me
the old woman cautioned: Bite off
her nails with your teeth
and bury them in the earth.

In the fall of that year
the feet of Abraham
went overhead—Isaac his son
at his side, the wood
for the burnt offering sprouting
leaves at one end, root hairs
at the other.
And the fire
in the father's hands
sent up its bright alphabet,
a signal to Sarah.

In the narrow passage between intent
and act,
the angel's call
and the confusion of the ram.

Here, on our side
in the Feast of Booths
the trees
have put out too much fruit
as though after the long drought
they might not survive: black walnuts,
acorns not yet ripe, tough capsules
propelled through the air
without letup;
the knobs leave their imprint
on the soles of our feet.

In the firmament
between worlds the guardian
of invalid prayers—those uttered
with the lips, the heart
dragging behind—urges us
to delay awhile.

What doors must close
before this one can open?
And which angel
rises up through the brickwork
of sapphire
to bid farewell
to this child torn out
of the distance
like the leaf of the ash I tear off
to find
in back of each green shape
a seed
trawling in the morning light.

Instructions for the Messiah

Do not think
you must work signs
and miracles
or resurrect the dead.

It is sufficient
that you have diligently
studied the law.
We would ask of you

only the rebuilding
of the temple
and the gathering in
of the exiles.

These will define you
and nothing will seem changed.
Night will follow day
as it always has.

It was never for dominion
that we invented you
but only that we might
return to our houses.

Inside
we would know
the hidden things
of this world.

WHAT IS A JEWISH POEM?

Does it wear a yarmulka
and tallis
does it live
in the diaspora
and yearn for homeland

Does it wave the lulav
to and fro inside
a plastic sukkah
or recite
the seven benedictions
under the chupah

I wonder
what is a Jewish poem
Does it only go to synagogue
one day a year
attaching the tfillin

like a tiny black stranger
to its left arm

Does it open
the stiff skins
of the prayerbook
to reveal the letters
like blackened platelets
twisting within

Little yeshiva bocher
little Jewish poem
waving your sidecurls
whispering piyyut to me
in my sleep

Little Jewish poem
in your shtreimel hat
little grandfather
sing to me
little Jewish poem
come sing to me

CERTAINTY

$\mathscr{I}$ have begun to forget the meaning of words. Arieh writes to me from his settlement in the south to say that the khamsin has come early. In autumn. I look at the word for a long time: autumn. Does it come before summer? Before spring? Autumn: dusk? Autumn. I have lost it. Its certainty. The way it once had an irrevocable meaning, its definition contained in it like a nucleus. It wears that definition loosely now, like a hat which blows off in the slightest wind.

Arieh is coming home. It is better to write of a thing before it happens. Afterward one must deal with the facts. But before, one can imagine the whole event, add to it, embellish it. Before, the events stretch out in all their possible forms. She wakes up, goes to the door, and finds him waiting there. Or, she is driving along the highway toward the north and his car passes hers. They stop to walk together along the wadi. They go a long way in silence. Or, she has just prepared the meal. And he comes in then. She takes his coat and sets him down to the table and serves him the cabbage and eggplant and tomatoes she has grown herself. The rosemary pointing up the flavor, the spokes of the herb like signals in the sauce.

Signals of warning? Autumn. The word has a buzz at the end that is felt at the back of the throat. The mouth opens on it and closes like the shell of a clam. Fall. In the northern hemisphere. In the southern hemisphere, that time from the March equinox to the June solstice. You see, each idea seemed perfectly clear once. Each word. Without conditions, without exceptions. Does the water in the tub drain out clockwise or counterclockwise? Which hemisphere is this, actually?

In the zone of the doldrums the wind has almost stopped altogether. Horses harnassed to the equator can no longer pull the earth in its orbit, so affected are they by the intense heat.

He writes that there are troop movements to the east. That they have had to rise early for two weeks to go on maneuvers. That the sudden inactivity has him worried. They cannot clear their heads during this time of the hot winds. They are irritable. He writes that there is a peculiar expectancy, the way a certain sound at a high frequency enters your consciousness and you suddenly become aware that your whole attention is fastened to it, that you have begun to wait for that moment when it will cease. Like pain.

It is not his custom to warn me of his arrivals. He likes a certain tension, a suspense about his comings and goings. I have grown to like that as well. And anyhow, it is a reminder that certainty is something we want, not a quality of this world, not of this life. For hasn't the old woman died without asking if we minded. Netka, how was it you didn't wait for me to come home, to come to your side that night? But just died, quietly, alone. And Chanah, after the weeks, a whole year at your side, you waited till I had gone home to my own bed to sleep before you relinquished this life. I arrived there that morning to find your face raised to the light, your mouth in a peaceful smile as though you had discovered something we weren't ever to know, as if you had gone over to a place we hadn't any business in. And anyway, what would I have done had I been there at that moment of leaving? Would it have been different?

Death. There's another one. Hearth, breath. Wreathe. Death. If I say it often enough, the word shakes off its meaning like the dust of the rug Semmel beats in his window, like the dress Yenne shakes, the slight shudder of her body inside. Only the thick feel of my tongue between my teeth when I come down on the final consonants, the muffling of sound like the cover of snow, like the blanket that covered Chanah's face that morning, when two strangers came to take her from the room.

At Eilat there is a hot wind that comes from Africa. When you breathe it in, your nostrils burn. Your bare arms feel hot to the touch. Though you are out of doors, between desert and sea, breathing itself brings a sense of claustrophobia.

The conversation begins as though it has never ended. As though he hadn't left. The odor of other places is on him. I try to decipher the geography of his passage. I make a map and I place him here, here. All the while he talks. I wonder if he has slept in the beds of other women. I wonder what they look like. He talks. I do not listen. Sometimes a word falls onto my plate. I pick it up idly on my fork and taste it. It is salty on the tip of my tongue. Another word. Sometimes bitter at the edges. At first I do not listen. It takes me a long while to gather up what was once between us, to take the words I have sent to others and call them in. Like a shepherd calling his flock at evening. I call them home so they can be his again.

I lay in the bed with my legs in the position of running. He on his side with his two arms in sleep out in front of him as though he were waiting to receive something. I imagine I am running down the stairs, turning off a light, washing clothes, cooking a meal. My thoughts race. Toward morning I turn to him, my breasts touch his back. I listen for the sound of his breathing which has become regular and deep. I try to imagine his dream. He turns toward me and I place my body between his outstretched arms.

CROSSING INTO THE

NEW MILLENNIUM

American University

Convocation, August 1998

*A*s we walk up the steep incline of the final years of this millennium, we have witnessed the staccato light from the tracers and antiaircraft fire above the ancient riverbeds that were our mothers and fathers ten thousand years ago—Iraq, the birthplace of the legal code of Hammurabi, the city of Nineveh. We have witnessed civil wars in many regions, brutalizing in ways we had dared to believe could not happen now. Events we did not expect to witness in our lifetime were compressed into weeks—the dismantling of the Berlin Wall, the Iron Curtain turned to filigree, as Eastern Europe, Russia opened. National borders changed, nations partitioned. There is a joke about the woman who goes to sleep one night in what was then Russia and wakes up in the morning in what is now Poland. "Oh," she says in the morning, "I'm so glad. I always hated those Russian winters.!"

We have witnessed the terrible brief utterance freedom makes when it takes up residence in those long suppressed and is crushed, as in Tiananmen Square; we have witnessed Nelson Mandela's walk to freedom after twenty-seven years' imprisonment.

The dislocation from imprisonment to freedom cannot be comprehended by ordinary means. Natan Sharansky, taken from the Gulag to Berlin, crossing the Berlin Wall into the free world in 1986—when some of you were only six years old—describes the "almost unbearable elation" as well as the nagging apprehension that this was "just another prison dream . . . that he would soon awake in a cold, brutalizing cell."

"Through seven mountain frontiers/ barbed wire of rivers/ . . . executed forests and hanged bridges/ I kept coming . . . / I hadn't a hope/ but I'm here . . . "[1] the Polish poet Zbigniew Herbert has written.

In the post–Cold War era, our real work has begun and all of you will be part of that work—to determine how the nations and their citizens will interact. We know already that national boundaries are no longer the sole determinants.

During your time at American University we will cross over together into the next millennium. I want to talk a little about our journey. Not the arrival. About how what we experience becomes to a large extent who we are. As the Argentine writer Borges wrote:

> Through the years, a man peoples a space with images of provinces, kingdoms, mountains, bays, ships, islands, fishes, rooms, tools, stars, horses, and people. Shortly before his death, he discovers that the patient labyrinth of lines traces the image of his own face.[2]

At times we do not understand how a certain direction we take will prove to be useful to us in the end, but we are drawn to that path. I have always believed it important to attend to such inclinations. Even if it meant that we would find out only years later just what that direction had to do with the main journey of our life.

I'd like to share a personal story. I was born before the advent of antibiotics. Because I was relatively frail as a child and often sick—there was essentially no treatment for strep infections or other upper respiratory illnesses. Sulfa drugs that were sometimes used caused me a major allergic reaction—and because rheumatic heart disease, caused by complications of untreated strep, was so prevalent in my childhood, I was essentially put to bed for weeks at a time. My mother's brother had died as a young adult of the complications of rheumatic heart disease. If memory serves, I would say that I attended school only a third of the time. When I was well enough to go outside again, but not well enough to return to school, I would spend my days playing alone in the woods— it was safe in those days for children to wander unattended out of doors—near my house, examining insects, tasting the inside of the bark of sassafras, eating sour grass, or I would sometimes go to work with my scientist father, something I loved to do. I remember pushing a tiny ball of mercury around on the floor, trying to gather it up from the cracks between oak planks, pressing a thumb down on the tiny bead and watching it break into minute celestial fragments. We did not worry about mercury poisoning in those days. Or I would watch great sheets of synthetic rubber being pressed through huge rollers (this was during the Second World War); I can still remember the odor in the pilot plant where experiments were conducted. I can see, in my mind's eye, the huge bluish glass reagent bottles containing HCL and other caustic liquids. The scientist's laboratory was as comfortable for me as any schoolroom.

During adolescence I worked summers in labs and majored in biology at college. Afterward I worked at Yale Medical School studying frontal lobe function and memory in Rhesus monkeys in the department of neurophysiology. Those were the days when Harry Harlow was doing his experiments with terrycloth mothers and the ability or failure of infant monkeys to thrive under varying conditions of nurture. When I went to collect my monkeys from their cages, I had to withstand the pouncing crazed chattering of Delgado's monkeys with implanted electrodes. I would pass Paul MacLean's monkeys during the years when he was making discoveries about the limbic system.

Years earlier I had worked in one of the largest warehouses for mental patients in the country, Central Islip State Hospital, where thousands of schizophrenics had been lobotomized. I was baffled and horrified by what had been done to these people to make them "tractable." I began to read about psychosurgery, Freeman and Watts's book on their early work in neurosurgery, and to think about how such treatment had become acceptable in our society. Later, in college, I studied neurophysiology taught by Kenneth Roeder, the kind of teacher whose influence on those he came in contact with brought many to the field.

During that period I also followed out an interest in molecular biology and studied at Cold Spring Harbor Biological Laboratory where, at the time, Salvador Luria, Max Delbruck, and others in the field were observing the ways in which viruses could redirect the genetic machinery of cells. The whole field of bacterial genetics was opening. In a sense, work in the 1950s was laying the groundwork for the enormous growth of knowledge that has been so essential for the field of immunology. Without that work we would have little understanding of the complex machinery of the HIV virus, for instance.

Somewhere along the way in my own journey, I paid attention to the fact that literature—poetry, fiction, essays, biography, what writers had to teach us—was the mainstay of my life. And I went back to school—a course at a time at first, and then to graduate school. And eventually it was time to cross the threshold from student to teacher. In 1970, during the Viet Nam war, when young men were returning and coming back to school, I started to teach here at American University.

It has always been my belief that whatever we have exposure to, whatever we learn in our lives is not wasted, but is only waiting to come into use. Of course we cannot ever use all that is within us. But what we are drawn to, much like what is now being called "potentiality" in the memory system, will eventually play a role in our mental life. Thus, all these years later, in my own life, it is the Holocaust in Lithuania that calls forth once more my old interest in memory and sends me in the direction of the neuroscientists to see what I can learn from them.

For years, parts of my life were partitioned off—here is the part about science; here is the part about literature; here is music; here is family. Like the specialists of earlier days, I can lift away the partitions that separate the parts of my life and attempt to use more of what I know in this new work.

What, you may be asking at this moment, does this have to do with me?

It is about the world and our relation to it—whether we come to know our world through art or science, through literature or international studies, through intuitive or analytical means. What shall be our tools for finding our way and contributing? How will our time at American University assist in our development? It would be an interesting exercise to write down in a journal what you expect of these years at the University, why you have come here to study, what you hope to learn—and then to see if, at the conclusion of your time here, your goals have changed, and if you feel that you have accomplished what you set out to do. In learning there is not always an immediate, visible demonstration of the benefits, just as in science practitioners must work for decades, at often very lonely work, before some spectacular discovery comes along that changes our lives. So with those who, behind the scenes, create art or music or literature. Years of isolated work are required.

You'll get a lot of advice while you are here. Some will be useful and some not. But here, for whatever it is worth, is mine.

Pay attention to what interests you. Though learning is a lifelong process, it is likely that never again in your lives will you have such years to devote so fully to learning.

As Dr. Ladner has said and as you know, we live in an extraordinary city. This was the home of poet/teacher Sterling Brown, historian Rayford Logan, physician W. Montague Cobb, the place where Langston Hughes, Zora Neale Hurston, Jean Toomer, Paul Laurence Dunbar, Toni Morrison, Duke Ellington, and many others lived and worked. Engage actively with what is here. There is not anything, not any area of our lives in the world that isn't dealt with here.

Learn from one another: you come from every corner of the earth and from all over the United States, bringing with you diverse cultures, languages, experiences.

Study deeply. Ask a great deal of yourself. You will be tempted—and rightly so—to respond actively to all the opportunities here in Washington. For many of you, it is the reason you have come to American. Be sure to include the *depth* of learning as part of your journey.

Take risks in learning, open doors, even to what may seem impossible. Did you know that Monarch butterflies migrate from eastern Canada to their wintering sites in Mexico, over a range of 4,500 kilometers, that those flimsy lovely creatures with poor vision, a limited capacity to learn, with difficulty regulating body temperature, a ridiculous rate of fuel consumption during powered flight, and a poor aerodynamic design—nothing to recommend them for long migrations—somehow make their way across the continent? If butterflies can do it, so can you make your way across the continent of knowledge.

Include proficiency in technology as part of your learning. "The Internet," as Dr. Rita Colwell, President of the NSF has said, "has imprinted all our lives much like a kind of societal DNA."

Call upon faculty, staff, administrators while you are here. The informal exchanges between faculty and student can be of singular importance in your intellectual development. Don't be afraid to take advantage of this opportunity.

Take a deep breath, enjoy one another, have some fun.

And remember the journey. Yes, it is important to set goals, to have a place in the future by which to measure the extent of your journey. Or as Ursula LeGuin has written: "It is good to have an end to journey toward, but in the end it is the journey that matters." Remember the words of the Greek poet Constantine Cavafy as he wrote about Homer's Odysseus and his struggle to get home to Ithaka after the fall of Troy. The narrator instructs us about the journey Odysseus made as well as about our own life journey. As you may recall, Odysseus took many years to arrive and along the way he had many adventures:

> When you set out for Ithaka
> ask that your way be long,
> full of adventure, full of instruction.
>   . . .
> Have Ithaka always in your mind.
> Your arrival there is what you are destined for.
> But do not in the least hurry the journey.
> Better that it last for years,
> so that when you reach the island you are old,
> rich with all you have gained on the way,
> not expecting Ithaka to give you wealth.
> Ithaka gave you the splendid journey.
> Without her you would not have set out.[3]

GRANDFATHER

Lost and Found

1

*O*n June 23, 1998, I found my grandfather. It wasn't that I had lost him. He died before I was born. 1932. I was given his name. As an old woman in Lithuania told me, the name means shining light. "Like your face," she said. But I did not know where my grandfather was born. Nor where he grew up. Oh, I knew the country. Lithuania. A place squeezed between powerful nations. The size of West Virginia, though once it covered the territory from the Baltic to the Black Sea.

My grandfather's ancestors had come to this place around the same time that its people were first discovering monotheism, the last of the nations to discover Christianity. A deeply religious man—one of the *mitnagdim* (the opponents of Hasidism)— found himself among those who once worshiped rivers and oak trees. I am told it was a rarity for Jews to have been farmers. They were forbidden to own land during Czarist times; yet my grandfather's parents owned their own land and farmed it. Perhaps they too belonged to the river and giant trees that bounded their land. The Susve River that flowed through the fertile valley of that region.

But where, I had wondered all my life, was he born, this Meir Aharon. My mother took quite seriously the injunction to name after the dead. She didn't bother to change the gender. I am Aharon. For her father. A man whom she didn't get to know until she was an adult. A man who thought that daughters were not to be educated, taking his five out of school at age thirteen to work, to help support the family. Like his village in Lithuania erased under Soviet times, they lived on a Washington street that no longer exists: 4½ Street, S.W.

2

June 23, 1998: We go, on this day, to the places of massacre. The first pogroms in Kaunas—1941. To Lietukis Garage where a young man and others grabbed Jews off the street and beat them to death with irons and clubs. Or using high pressure hoses pumped water into them until they exploded. The others bring flowers to these places. They say prayers for the dead in Hebrew, prayers that never mention the word *death*. Holy and magnified, starts the prayer, is the Lord. Why so holy and magnified? Why not a God who stops such things? And why thank him in this way? Why not say: God who failed us. God who isn't at home. God who is blind and deaf and mute—*that* God. They stop at the Fort VII and place flowers there. And again the prayer. There are not even enough men for a minyan. They must say the prayer without ten men. I cannot help. I am no substitute for a man, even with my man's name. Though I offer.

3

I have circled this place, round and round. For five years. Even in these two weeks, still without knowing. I returned to Josvainiai, to Krakes, to Babtai, drawn by the small wooden houses, by the barking dogs—more wolf than dog—tied with rope in the yards. Drawn by the wooden hay wagons, handheld plows, a fly swatter made of a long branch and a flared piece of rubber lying on a wooden sill, like an implement from the Middle Ages. Drawn by the pile of dried beans, talking and shelling the ghostly white beans for winter. By the ceramic stoves, large enough to warm a whole family in winter. Drawn by houses with three windows in front. Jewish houses, I am told.

It was not that I could have imagined where to place this grandfather. For without knowing him, I could not judge where he might have lived. But I knew his wife, my grandmother. In many ways, my mother. Or the mother I aspired to be. The earthy mystery of her kitchen—dough rising in an enamel pan on the radiator, the tiny golden moons of unfertilized eggs from the chickens, the hairpin and cork she used to remove the stones from cherries that she preserved. Braiding her beautiful dark hair each night before sleeping. And after her death, my sisters and I wrapped in her comforting flannel nightgowns.

Like the women survivors in Lithuania. Their beautiful Yiddish. Like the Lithuanian women in their eighties. Like Aleksandra Balandiene in Datnuva who first ran after our car in 1993, crying after us until we opened the car door and invited her in. And the miracle is, she did come in to talk with strangers. Perhaps she thought we were survivors returning to claim our houses, our lives in her town. They say it was our family town—so many of us lived there then. Someday I must ask her why she ran after us that day.

She speaks Yiddish and Polish, Russian, Lithuanian, German. The Jews, she tells us, spoke Hebrew in order not to be understood by the Lithuanians. One day, I was sitting on the small wooden chair in her living room when she suddenly stopped talking and looked at me. "You look like . . ." she paused, "Leah Lopaiko." A name I would never have asked about. My mother's first cousin. Long dead. Escaped to Russia during the mass killings in this town where no Jew who remained survived. Returned briefly after the war. Was it possible that I could bear enough resemblance to this person that we could close the enormous distance? But it was confirmation enough. Not a soul could have known that name who had not known her personally. Aleksandra had been close to my family before the war. She had visited their home, had attended synagogue services during family celebrations. Leah's brother Shimon, she reminded me, had a red birthmark on his face. "Do you know what has happened to them? she wanted to know.

"Our Father," Aleksandra tells us, when she speaks of her husband. But last year, when I return to her, her head is covered with a black kerchief. I am always afraid that she will be gone, that her life will be over and I will not find her anymore in this tiny village. And then it will be that my link through her will become invisible. Like the objects of my mother that seemed to relinquish their life once she was no longer alive. As long as Aleksandra is alive, so do my cousins live in Datnuva. As long as she can tell stories about them.

We cannot console her this time: she speaks of her longing to go and lie down in the graveyard next to her husband. She can see his grave from her window. I ask if she will sing something. She goes to find her Bible and begins: "Maria, Maria . . ." For days and weeks and months, I hold the tape recorder to my ear and I sing with her: "Mar . . . i . . . a, Mar . . . i . . . a." I only find out now, on this day of America's Independence, that when the Lithuanians were hauled off to Siberia by the hundreds and thousands, they sang this beautiful, sad song. It begins this way:

Marija! Marija!
Skaisčiausia lelija!
Tu švieti aukštai ant Dangaus!
Palengvink vergija!
Išgelbek nuo priešo baisaus!
Mes, klystantys žmonès,
Maldaujam malones;

Mary, Mary,
You luminous lily,
You shine in the heavens on high.
Alleviate servitude
Assist humanity
Save us from terrible foes.
. . .
Mary, Mary,
Luminous lily,
Bright queen of heaven,
Intercede with the Highest
On behalf of the lowest
For God will listen to you.

4

On the way to the grandfather, how many fields have I crossed, how many wetlands sunken into, how many cemetery stones searched, how many villages, haystacks, how many questions. On the way to the grandfather I have walked the perimeter of the massacre places. Scrawling along the edge, like a margin around the bodies. The sacred letters are sleeping within the burial mound, the tumuli where they were thrown, some still alive. The quivering earth moving for days. On the way to the grandfather, some saw the red mist for the first time in their lives. And the man whose property this was claimed not to be at home when the killings took place. But others knew better. Even his children told the truth. On the way to the grandfather, such a man gave up sleeping in his house and came to the earth to pass his nights. But even that did not help. And he went mad with the murders done on his land. And with his consent.

5

The grandfather was not lost. And he was not found. I had never known him. In America with her brimming streets and her fast talkers, it is difficult to make the journey to these places. We are all optimism. We have many lives, little past. Abundant futures. Chances. Even the hardest lives have that. Even the lost children. In what languages to say these things? By chance I am in Lithuania during the days of commemoration. Here is the house of Rabbi Ossowsky, his body found bent over the page of the Talmud he was studying, his severed head propped in the window like a talisman.

Many are the false destinations on the way to the grandfather, but each prepares the traveler for the next. Whether along the heated stony earth of a mountain village in Evvoia or in the far reaches of the Sahara Desert where Jews who resemble nothing more than our Biblical patriarchs still reside. It is always toward the rural village that I seem to travel. Ruseiniai in the District of Yosvainiai in the Province of Kaunas and in the Kedainiai region. Alongside the Susve River. My grandfather, the document read, was to be conscripted into military service. The date is December 22, 1889. It is too late. He has already left for America. Though it is not too late to punish his family left behind. A fine of 300 rubles.

By now my grandfather is somewhere in America, in West Virginia, on a horse and wagon selling biscuits and stopping to pray in the barns of farmers. Perhaps they thought it strange to see this Jew with his prayer shawl and yarmalkah, but now I understand why he might have felt at home among barns, among wagons and fields.

The village of Ruseiniai is near an old Lithuanian cemetery, the only marker to indicate that once there was a village here. It is not on any map. Yocheved, my friend, arranges to take me there. We head toward Josvainiai and to Angiriai in the direction of Krakes. Ruseiniai is a little over 1 kilometre northwest of Angiriai on the east side of the Susve River. The document reads: Meir Aharon Wolpe, son of Elieser Tsemach, farmers. In the cemetery, I kneel in the field, among the wild asters and tall grasses. I pick flowers for my two sisters that I will press between the pages of a book of Lithuanian poetry to bring to them.

Meyer Aharon Wolpe (author's grandfather) and Anne Wolpe Weisberg (author's mother) circa 1913, in Washington, D.C. Photographer unknown.

ODE TO THE CZAR'S ASSASSIN

1

I sing of the Czar's
assassin, of his knife,

of the delicate thread
he winds three times

around the neck
of Czar Alexander the Second.

I sing to the words he whispers
as he helps Alexander

take his last breath.
It is to him I owe my life.

2

I thank the Czar's assassin
for scaring my little grandmother,

for sending her flying with her feather
bed and a few metal pots

and pans into the new world.
I sing to Czar Alexander's

mother who foolishly
entrusted her child to a poet—

Vasily Zhukovsky who wrapped him
in verses and trained him

to be gentle. Alas, see how poetry
can ruin a man!

3

I sing to Alexander
who took the silver tracks

that carried his people from Moscow
to Petersburg and stretched

them across the world, rail lines opening
outward like his freed people.

That is how he let my little
grandmother begin to dream.

4

I sing to the Czar's assassin
for reminding her

to be afraid. I sing
to my grandmother's fear,

to her snail's antennae
that sniffed the dangerous

air of Lithuania, to her mother
who packed a wicker

basket so full
three strong men had to carry it.

I sing to the useless
items she dragged from the old world

to the new, to embroidered bedsheets,
hairpins, to delicate cups

and saucers that would break
along the way, to feathers

plucked one
by one that would gather beads

of moisture and sink
to the bottom of the wicker basket.

                    5
I sing to my grandmother's
high-bottoned shoes,

to her old legs when I knelt
before her years later

and pulled at the layers
of rubber stockings like bark

on a tree. I sing
to the child whose fear

took her away from the oak trees,
the beloved language

the rivers and fields
of her life.

6

I praise the Czar's assassin
who kept me from being bones

in the graveyard, blood earth
in the massacre pit

provender for the sacred oaks.
I would have been birch

or flax, rye seed in their bread, spore
in their mushroom, wild

strawberry, filament
of hair, cry for help scratched

into the wall of the Czar's fortress
or cell in the great wash

of their Nieman their Neris—twin
rivers pulling at the shore.

7

I sing to the Czar's assassin
for not letting

my grandmother feel at home
in Lithuania.

For giving me my life, so I could, one day,
return to the rivers, the stones,

to the earth of her childhood
that reaching across

the landscape of my mother's body
I could walk in my grandmother's steps.

THE MESSIAH RECONSIDERED

1
How often
and in what detail
we have imagined you.

Like the fine blades
of grass, the attention
to each wing petal
of the angel da Vinci made.

This is the way
we have counted off
the years
of your absence.

Weren't we warned
how blindness

does not imply
darkness.

So your absence
is composed of valleys,
of fiery delegations.

2

Oh all the armies
of messiahs—we are hemmed
in by them: a Cretan,
later a Persian who claimed
to have found
the Ten Lost Tribes.

One nearly
took hold—born
on the eve of the exile
to Babylon.

Sabbatai Zevi
who descended the husks
to redeem scattered
sparks of divine light.

3

Not much is said
of Sarah the orphaned
survivor he married.

Perhaps she lived
many years
like her namesake
and bore him a son
in her old age.

Her husband
the messiah
converted to Islam.

4

Some of us say:
He has come.
See he lives here
among us.

Others tell
of the rabbi who slept
without undressing
six of the seven nights
of the week
in order to be ready
to greet him.
On the seventh
he took off his clothes:
sabbath is holier
than redemption.

5

What riddle
do we with our few days
make of our messiah—
That there is
no body lighter
than water?
How could he have walked
on the surface
like these words walking
on stilts
across the white page?

That there could be
between us this absence—
the comforting
conjunction of grooved
entablature, creases
in a band that rounds
the beloved head.

That we are not immune
from dreaming of him
like the shepherds
who looked up.

That we must
come back each year into
the vicinity
of our longing, back
to the neighborhood of
the possible.

$\mathcal{N}otes$

LEARNING THE LANGUAGE

1. Stanley Burnshaw, T. Carmi, and Ezra Spicehandler, eds., in *The Modern Hebrew Poem Itself*, Trans. by T. Carmi (New York: Schocken Books, 1971), p. 136.

2. Ibid., p. 138.

3. "HaMatmid," in *Selected Poems of Hayyim Nahman Bialik*, ed. Israel Efros (New York: Bloch Publishing Company, 1965), p. 29.

4. Aharon Megged, "How Did the Bible Put It," *Encounter Magazine* (1971).

5. Ibid.

6. Burnshaw et al., *Modern Hebrew Poem*, p. 169.

7. All quoted passages in this essay are taken from Isaac Singer's *The Magician of Lublin* (New York: The Noonday Press/Farrar, Straus and Giroux, 1967) and *The Slave* (New York: Farrar, Straus and Cudahy, 1962).

8. Poems in this essay by Glatstein and Sutzkever appear in *The Penguin Book of Modern Yiddish Verse*, ed. Irving Howe, Ruth Wisse, and Khone Shmeruk (New York: Viking, 1987).

THE WORLD IS A PARCHMENT SCRAWLED WITH WORDS

1. Moshe Dor, *Khamsin: Memoirs and Poetry by a Native Israeli* (Colorado Springs, Colo.: Three Continents Press, 1994); Preface, "Khamsin," by Myra Sklarew.

2. Hayim Nahman Bialik, "Cedars of Lebanon: Revealment and Concealment in Language," *Commentary* 9, no. 2 (February 1950): 171–75. All references to Bialik in Myra Sklarew's preface to *Night Watch* by Barbara Goldberg can be found in this essay.

191

3. Barbara Goldberg, *Night Watch,* trans. into Hebrew by Moshe Dor. (Tel Aviv: Keshev Publishing House, 2001).

4. Linda Grey Sexton and Lois Ames, eds., *Anne Sexton: A Self-Portrait in Letters* (Boston: Houghton Mifflin, 1977) pp. 59, 120.

5. John Holmes, ed., *A Little Treasury of Love Poems: From Chaucer to Dylan Thomas* (New York: Charles Scribner's Sons, 1950) pp. 167–68.

6. Ibids., *Writing Poetry* (Boston: The Writer, Inc., 1960).

7. This was later printed as "Surroundings and Illuminations," in *A Celebration of Poets* edited by Don Cameron Allen (Baltimore: The Johns Hopkins University Press, 1967) pp. 108–30.

8. John Holmes, *The Fortune Teller* (New York: Harper & Brothers, 1961), pp. 3–4, 11.

9. Ibid., *The Double Root* (New York: Twayne Publishers, 1950).

10. Jorge Luis Borges, *Labyrinths: Selected Stories & Other Writings* (New York: New Directions, 1964) p. 51.

11. Stephen Henderson, *Understanding the New Black Poetry: Black Speech and Black Music as Poetic References* (New York: William Morrow, 1973) pp. 184–85.

12. Eugene Redmond, *Drumvoices: the Mission of Afro-American Poetry: A Critical History* (Garden City: Anchor Press, 1976).

13. For the twenty-page anthology of poems by the Howard Poets that was originally included with this essay, see *The Washington Review,* 15 February 1978. WAMU-FM broadcast a program on 8 February 1978 on the Howard Poets with readings by Lance Jeffers and others.

14. Edwin Honig, *Garcia Lorca* (Norfolk, Conn.: New Directions Books, 1944) pp. 59–60. The poem "Agosto" by Federico Garcia Lorca is presented in Spanish and in English translation by Edwin Honig, though I no longer recall who has translated the version I have used in this essay. It may well have been done with the help of my students.

15. Lawrence Raab, *Mysteries of the Horizon* (New York: Doubleday, 1972) p. 56–57.

LIFE, THE UNFINISHED EXPERIMENT

This section takes its title from a book by a leading researcher in the field of bacterial genetics and bacterial viruses, Salvador E. Luria's *Life, The Unfinished Experiment.* Nobel Laureate Luria was a pioneer in the field of molecular biology and teacher of James Watson who helped to decipher the structure of the DNA molecule. I was fortunate to have studied with him at Cold Spring Harbor Biological Laboratory one remarkable summer (1955) when the mechanisms by which viruses could enter a cell and redirect its genetic machinery were first being understood. At the time I was eager to complete college in fewer than four years by taking courses in bacterial genetics and viruses in order to marry. I had barely a hint then that this subject would continue to fascinate me for the rest of my life.

1. Julio Cortazar, "Preamble to the Instructions on How to Wind a Watch," *Cronopios and Famas* (New York: Random House, 1969), pp.23–24.

2. Richard Dawkins, *The Selfish Gene* (New York: Oxford University Press, 1978).

3. L. H. Finkel, "The Construction of Perception," in *Incorporations,* ed. J. Crary and S. Kwinter, *Zone,* Vol. 6, (New York; Urzone Inc., 1992). See also L. H. Finkel, "Constructing Visual Perception," *American Scientist* 82 (1994):224–37, for an additional discussion by this very original researcher.

4. See Carla Shatz, remarks at the White House Conference on Early Childhood Development and Learning, 17 April 1997, (http://www.dana.org /dabi/carlashatz.html). See also C. J. Shatz, "Wiring the Brain" in *Useful Knowledge,* ed. Alexander G. Bearn (Philadelphia: American Philosophical Society, 1999), pp. 89–97.

5. Gustav Eckstein, *The Body Has a Head* (New York: Harper & Row, 1970), p. 568.

6. This essay is based upon an interview with Dr. Steven Rosenberg at the National Institutes of Health under the auspices of Professor Barbara Culliton's course on Writing Science at The Johns Hopkins University.

7. Thomas E. Starzl, *The Puzzle People: Memoirs of a Transplant Surgeon* (Pittsburgh: University of Pittsburgh Press, 1993).

8. David G. Nathan, *Genes, Blood, and Courage: A Boy Called Immortal Sword* (Cambridge: Harvard University Press, 1995).

9. George Steiner, *After Babel: Aspects of Language and Translation* (New York and London: Oxford University Press, 1975).

10. This essay, written ten years ago, could only begin to presage the important current debate on the use of embryonic stem cells and their potential for treating a number of human diseases.

11. Sigmund Freud, *MetaPsychological Supplement to the Theory of Dreams, The Standard Edition of the Complete Psychological works of Sigmund Freud,* Vol. 14, (London: The Hogarth Press, 1917), p. 222.

12. François Jacob, *The Statue Within* (New York: Basic Books, 1988).

A PLACE CALLED GEHINOM

1. Norma Rosen, *Accidents of Influence* (Albany: SUNY Press, 1992).

2. See *The Einsatzgruppen Reports,* edited by Yitzhak Arad, Shmuel Krakowski, and Shmuel Spector (New York: Holocaust Library, 1989) and Masha

Greenbaum's *The Jews of Lithuania* (New York: Gefen Books 1995). See "Total list of the Executions carried out in the Area of Einstazkommando 3 by 1 December 1941," Office of Special Investigations, U.S. Department of Justice.

3. Theodor Adorno, "Commitment" in *The Essential Frankfurt School Reader,* edited by Andrew Arato and Elke Gebhardt (New York: Continuum, 1982).

4. From an introduction to the author at the Library of Congress's Poetry and Literature Series, 13 November 1977, by Robert Pinsky, Poet Laureate.

5. From a manuscript, "Israel and the Eichmann Trial," 1963, by Paul Danaceau with permission of the author.

6. Charlotte Delbo, *Days and Memory* (Marlboro, V.: The Marlboro Press, 1990).

7. Jean Amery, *At the Mind's Limits* (Bloomington: Indiana University Press, 1980).

8. Michael Steinlauf, *Bondage to the Dead: Poland and the Memory of the Holocaust* (Syracuse, N.Y.: Syracuse University Press, 1997).

9. Yocheved Inciuriene, "Isgyventi Per Vokieciu Okupacija Lietuvoje," in *Baltos Lankos #5* (literal translation by George Birman).

10. Chaim Grade, "Sanctuaries in Ruin," in *Great Yiddish Writers of the Twentieth Century,* ed. Joseph Leftwich (New Jersey/London: Jason Aronson, 1987).

11. William Kincade and G. E. Schafft, "Holes in Their Histories: Public History and Public Policy," *International Studies Notes of the International Studies Association* 18, 2 (Spring 1993): 6–14.

12. Simon Schama, *Landscape and Memory* (New York: Alfred A. Knopf, 1995).

13. Phillip Hallie, *Lest Innocent Blood Be Shed* (New York: Harper & Row, 1979).

INSTRUCTIONS FOR THE MESSIAH

1. Zbigniew Herbert, *Selected Poems* (Baltimore: Penguin Books, 1968), pp. 85–87.

2. Jorge Luis Borges, *A Personal Anthology,* from the "Editor's Epilogue," (New York: Grove Press, 1967), from the p. 203.

3. Constantine Cavafy, *Six Poets of Modern Greece* (New York: Alfred A. Knopf, 1968) pp. 36–37.

Index of Names

Adorno, Theodor, 136–137
Akhmatova, Anna, 137
Akiba, R., 38
Allen, Sam, 89–90
Alvarez de Toledo, Letizia, 77
Amery, Jean, 140–141
Amichai, Yehuda, 11–12, 14
Asch, Sholem, 145
Auden, W. H., 79, 81, 83–85

Balandiene, Aleksandra, 178
Bar Yochai, Shimon, 30
Beckett, Samuel, 83–84
Ben Moshe Sebbagh, Mordechai, 29
Benjamin, Walter, 143
Beth Hillel, 55
Bialik, Hayim Nahman, 6, 12–13, 65–66
Blackiston, Lester, 91
Blackmur, R. P., 71
Blalock, Alfred, 115
Bloch, Chana, 25–26
Bonfiglio, Jon, 95
Borges, Jorge Luis, 77, 95, 171
Brodsky, Joseph, 79–88
Brooks, Gwendolyn, 89
Brown, Sterling, 89–91, 174
Brown, Claude, 91
Brown, Clifford, 92
Browne, Thomas, 122
Brueghel, 19

Caesar, Julius, 77
Callimachus, 77

Carmi, T., 5, 11, 14–16
Cavafy, Constantine, 175
Celan, Paul, 140, 148, 152
Chaucer, 70
Chetrit, Joseph, 30
Chetrit, Yacout, 30–31
Chmielnicki, 21
Ciardi, John, 70, 74
Cobb, W. Montague, 174
Coleman, Elliott, 72
Colwell, Rita, 174
Cooley, Thomas, 118
Cortazar, Julio, 95, 101
Cousens, John, 73
Crick, Francis, 128
Cullen Countee, 90
Curie, Madame, 78
Cushing, Harvey, 115
Czar Alexander II, 182

Dabney, Dick, 91
Danaceau, Paul, 139
Dante Alighieri, 70, 84, 87, 104
Darwin, Charles, 38, 102, 122, 125
Davis, Miles, 89, 92
Davis, Arthur P., 89
Dawkins, Richard, 101–102, 107
Dayem, 118-119
De Born, Bertrand, 104
Delbo, Charlotte, 140
Delbruck, Max, 128, 172
DeLegall, Walt, 89, 91
Delgado, 172
Dodson, Owen, 90–91

195